A Malaysian school becomes
a deadly battleground

The
Executioner®
Don Pendleton's
RAW FURY

DEMOCRACY HAS A FACE....

The
Don Pendleton's
Executioner®

An all-new Executioner
title every month!
Get in on the action!
Available at your
favorite retail outlet,
only from

GOLD EAGLE®

EAN

ISBN-13:978-0-373-64383-7

50499

GMBIFC3

A grenade bounced down the alley toward them

Without hesitating, Rosli stepped forward and planted a firm toe-kick with impeccable accuracy. The grenade whipped back the way it had come.

"Down!" Bolan ordered.

They hit the deck. The grenade exploded in the alley mouth. Bolan counted to three, his ears ringing from the blast, then surged up with the Beretta 93-R in both hands.

He advanced on the alley mouth. The bodies of the shooters he and Rosli had already killed were splayed in gruesome wreckage, torn by the explosion. Bolan had seen enough carnage in his lengthy personal war that the sight did not unnerve him, but he would never truly be used to it; no sane human being ever became completely inured to death and destruction. The Executioner simply did what he had to do, and took in measured stride the dead men he left in his wake—men who tried to take his life, or the lives of good men, women and children. If at some time Mack Bolan was held to account, if his tally were to be judged, he would stand unafraid before whatever power that might be.

But that day of judgment would not be this day.

MACK BOLAN ®
The Executioner

The Executioner®
Don Pendleton's

RAW FURY

A GOLD EAGLE BOOK FROM

WORLDWIDE®

TORONTO • NEW YORK • LONDON
AMSTERDAM • PARIS • SYDNEY • HAMBURG
STOCKHOLM • ATHENS • TOKYO • MILAN
MADRID • WARSAW • BUDAPEST • AUCKLAND

If you purchased this book without a cover you should be aware that this book is stolen property. It was reported as "unsold and destroyed" to the publisher, and neither the author nor the publisher has received any payment for this "stripped book."

Recycling programs
for this product may
not exist in your area.

First edition October 2010

ISBN-13: 978-0-373-64383-7

Special thanks and acknowledgment to
Phil Elmore for his contribution to this work.

RAW FURY

Copyright © 2010 by Worldwide Library.

All rights reserved. Except for use in any review, the reproduction or utilization of this work in whole or in part in any form by any electronic, mechanical or other means, now known or hereafter invented, including xerography, photocopying and recording, or in any information storage or retrieval system, is forbidden without the written permission of the publisher, Worldwide Library, 225 Duncan Mill Road, Don Mills, Ontario, Canada M3B 3K9.

This is a work of fiction. Names, characters, places and incidents are either the product of the author's imagination or are used fictitiously, and any resemblance to actual persons, living or dead, business establishments, events or locales is entirely coincidental.

® and TM are trademarks of the publisher. Trademarks indicated with ® are registered in the United States Patent and Trademark Office, the Canadian Trade Marks Office and in other countries.

Printed in U.S.A.

They have not wanted peace at all; they have wanted to be spared war—as though the absence of war was the same as peace.

—Dorothy Thompson
1893–1961

It has been said that if you want peace, you must prepare for war. To be prepared for armed conflict is not enough, however. To live in peace, we must have the will to fight.

—Mack Bolan

THE
MACK BOLAN
LEGEND

Nothing less than a war could have fashioned the destiny of the man called Mack Bolan. Bolan earned the Executioner title in the jungle hell of Vietnam.

But this soldier also wore another name—Sergeant Mercy. He was so tagged because of the compassion he showed to wounded comrades-in-arms and Vietnamese civilians.

Mack Bolan's second tour of duty ended prematurely when he was given emergency leave to return home and bury his family, victims of the Mob. Then he declared a one-man war against the Mafia.

He confronted the Families head-on from coast to coast, and soon a hope of victory began to appear. But Bolan had broken society's every rule. That same society started gunning for this elusive warrior—to no avail.

So Bolan was offered amnesty to work within the system against terrorism. This time, as an employee of Uncle Sam, Bolan became Colonel John Phoenix. With a command center at Stony Man Farm in Virginia, he and his new allies—Able Team and Phoenix Force—waged relentless war on a new adversary: the KGB.

But when his one true love, April Rose, died at the hands of the Soviet terror machine, Bolan severed all ties with Establishment authority.

Now, after a lengthy lone-wolf struggle and much soul-searching, the Executioner has agreed to enter an "arm's-length" alliance with his government once more, reserving the right to pursue personal missions in his Everlasting War.

1

Mack Bolan felt sweat bead on his chest and under his arms as the tropical heat of Kuala Lumpur struck him with palpable force. Temperatures were up slightly, according to the canned news reports televised in the main terminal, but while Bolan found the high nineties a bit on the warm side, it wasn't unbearable. The change was a shock after the air-conditioning of the airport, but the day's highs would not vary much in the city's year-round equatorial climate. If the operation went as planned, for that matter, he wouldn't be in Malaysia long enough to care.

He was glad to leave the frustrating congestion of the airport and picked up his pace accordingly. Glancing at his watch, he verified that he was still on schedule. The operation was tight, because it had to be. He had been aware of the numbers falling for the entire flight from the United States.

Bolan was dressed for the climate in a pair of tan cargo pants, lightweight hiking boots and a loose, short-sleeved khaki shirt that billowed about him in the humid breeze. It was bright outside the terminal; he took a pair of mirrored, aviator-framed sunglasses from his shirt pocket and put them on.

The man known to some as the Executioner ignored the insistent clerks behind the taxi counter, knowing that other arrangements had already been made for him. Bolan allowed himself a small, tight smile as he imagined their dismay. He was no stranger to the taxi scams outside Kuala Lumpur's International Airport, or outside the airports in dozens of other countries around the globe. Had he been left to his own devices, the Express Rail Link might have been an option, but he'd been warned to avoid that, too.

Outside the terminal, a line of taxis waited. Bolan glanced at his watch again. It was exactly two in the afternoon.

As if on cue, a battered, livery-marked Hyundai separated itself from the queue and roared around the lead vehicle to stop directly in front of Bolan. The car was dragging its muffler behind it, but the driver seemed not to notice. Behind him, the cabbie whose fare had just been stolen leaned on his horn, shouting a stream of what were probably profanities. Bolan did not speak the language but assumed it was Malay. Then the driver switched to English, leaving no doubt in the soldier's mind as to the man's intentions. Bolan remembered something from the tourism pamphlets on the flight; English was taught commonly in Malaysian schools.

"Get in, get in," the driver said, leaning toward the open passenger window. "Your friend Hal says hello."

Bolan got into the passenger seat. The taxi growled as the driver put the accelerator to the floor, causing the little car to shudder and buck as it pulled away from the outraged cabbie in the rearview mirror.

"And you are?" Bolan raised an eyebrow as his driver

pushed the Hyundai through the dense city traffic, cutting off other drivers with reckless abandon.

"You may call me Rosli," he said. His English was excellent, with just a hint of an accent. "You are Mr. Cooper, yes?"

"Yes," Bolan nodded. Matt Cooper was a cover identity he frequently used.

Rosli was of slight build, with a shaved head and a dark complexion. Deep laugh lines made him look older than he probably was. He wore a pair of lightly tinted, round sunglasses, a loose, beige, short-sleeved shirt and a pair of knee-length shorts. Bolan caught a glimpse of his sandaled feet as the man tromped the accelerator for all he was worth.

They drove in silence for a while, Bolan taking in the cityscape. He could see the glass-shelled Petronas Towers in the distance, at one time the tallest buildings in the world. The city was a mix of modern and postmodern architecture, with a healthy dose of nineteenth- and twentieth-century Colonial mixed in.

"I am surprised," Rosli said finally, "that you are so trusting. I was led to believe you were…a dangerous man. How do you know I am not sent to, what is the word…*waylay* you?"

"If you were," Bolan said casually, "I'd kill you, take the wheel and use the curb to bring the car to a stop."

Rosli opened his mouth to say something, caught something in Bolan's expression and thought better of it. Finally, he laughed. "Fair enough, Mr. Cooper," he chuckled. "Fair enough. I do believe you would, too."

Bolan did not comment.

"We will be at the school within ten minutes, depending on the traffic," Rosli said, darting around a small panel truck. "There is no time to waste. Your airdrop could not have come too soon."

"I wouldn't call a commercial flight an air drop," Bolan said.

"First class," Rosli said, "and faster than we could have arranged a charter."

"Luck," Bolan said.

"Providence," Rosli said with a grin. "And therefore the same thing. Regardless, we shall have you in place as quickly as possible, which is not soon enough. You will find what you requested under your seat. You will be pleased to see that everything is there. It was not easy. Your request was very specific. Very difficult."

Bolan nodded. He reached under the passenger seat to retrieve the olive-drab canvas messenger bag hidden there. He put it on his lap, below the level of the passenger-side windowsill, and inspected the contents.

The bag contained a Beretta 93-R machine pistol. There was also a stainless steel .44 Magnum Desert Eagle. A sound-suppressor and a leather shoulder-harness rig for the Beretta, several loaded magazines and a KYDEX inside-the-waistband holster for the Desert Eagle rounded out the bag's contents. The Executioner checked the action of one pistol, then the other, before loading both weapons and chambering live rounds. He set both guns on his lap.

In one of the outer pockets of the bag, Bolan found a locking stiletto with a six-inch blade. He pocketed the knife and shrugged into the shoulder harness under his shirt, holstering the Beretta and clipping the Desert Eagle in its holster behind his right hip. He slung the bag across his body, where it could hang on his left side.

Rosli had watched all this activity with interest. "You are impressively armed, Mr. Cooper," he said. "I am told the weapons were test-fired yesterday, and all is in order."

Bolan again made no comment. Either the guns would work or they wouldn't. He didn't like fielding gear untested by him or the Farm's armorer, John "Cowboy" Kissinger, but there was nothing to be done about it and no time not to do it. Mentally shrugging, he looked at Rosli and inclined his chin. When the Malaysian operative offered nothing, Bolan said, "And you?"

"A revolver, by my belt buckle," Rosli said, shrugging. "It is enough."

"It might be," Bolan said grudgingly. "It might not. That's going to depend."

"On what?" Rosli asked.

"Your proximity to *me*," the soldier said frankly.

"Ah." Rosli nodded, grinning widely through crooked but bright, white teeth. "Yes, that is as your friend Hal warned me it would be."

Bolan could imagine the exchange the big Fed might have had with Rosli, whom Brognola had described as a CIA asset of some sort, a local boy in long-distance employ of Central Intelligence. Bolan's own hurried conversation with Hal Brognola had taken place by phone only scant hours before, most of it occurring as Bolan was racing to make the international flight that was, simply by good fortune, scheduled to leave within the half hour. Had Bolan not been concluding some…business…in New York City that put him within a breakneck cab ride to JFK, he'd never have made it. As it was, the hundred dollars he'd tipped the cabbie before the ride had gotten him to the airport with no time to spare despite his near-suicidal driver's most earnest efforts.

"Striker," Brognola had said, using Bolan's code

name, "you're needed in Malaysia. Are you still in New York?"

When Bolan had acknowledged that, yes, he was, Brognola had asked him to catch the nearest cab as fast as he could for the airport, telling the soldier he would explain on the way.

"Okay, you've got my attention, Hal," Bolan had told him, hanging on for all he was worth as his taxi driver burned rubber while weaving in and out of traffic. "I'm on my way."

"There's a hostage situation in Kuala Lumpur," Brognola had explained. "An exclusive private school. It was seized by guerillas today."

"That sounds bad, Hal—" Bolan nodded, even though the big Fed couldn't see him and the very focused cabbie couldn't hear him and wouldn't care "—but that also sounds like a local problem."

"It would be," Brognola said, sounding tired. "But nothing is ever that simple, these days. Have you heard of—" Brognola paused, then recited as if reading from something "—Dato Seri Aswan Fahzal bin Abdul Tuan?"

Bolan blinked. To Brognola, he said, "I can't say I have."

"He's the prime minister of Malaysia," Brognola said. "Dato Seri is his title. Abdul Tuan was his father, if it matters."

"So this…Aswan Fahzal, is it?" Bolan said. "What's his connection?"

"He's referred to as just Fahzal, usually," Brognola said. "He swept into power last year amid a flurry of jingoistic fervor, as the media like to call it. His Nationalist Party has some pretty nasty overtones. 'Malaysia for Malaysians,' that kind of thing."

"Understood," Bolan said, his jaw clenching slightly.

"Well, Fahzal's government has been putting pressure on Malaysia's ethnic Indian and Chinese populations, of which there are significant numbers," Brognola continued. "It started slowly and was initially dismissed as caste-system politics or simple government favoritism. When it got worse, people started to complain, in the United Nations and on the international grassroots scene. I know the folks involved tried to get the attention of Amnesty International, among others."

"Did they?" Bolan asked.

"Not to the satisfaction of a very vicious few, apparently," Brognola said. "A new and violent Malaysian rebel group has risen up over the last, oh, six months. The members call themselves what translates roughly to something like, 'Birth Rights.' The Farm tagged the group 'BR' for simplicity's sake, because a few of the international terrorist-tracking groups call it that. The Malaysian government has taken to calling it that, too, for the sake of convenience, if nothing else, at least when they refer to it in English. I couldn't say about the Malay translation."

"I'm with you so far," Bolan said.

"BR has claimed responsibility for taking and holding the school," Brognola said. "If history is any guide, this will not end well. BR may claim to have noble goals, but its members have shown themselves to be terrorists. They've staged dozens of actions over the past few months, and in each case, innocents have died, and died hard. Lots of those have been children. BR likes to target young people to make the parents pay. It hasn't hit the international news because Fahzal's government has covered it up, suppressed it in the local media, but word has filtered out through other channels."

"You said BR has taken a school."

"I did. Among the VIPs who have children in that school is the prime minister himself. His son, Jawan, was the explicit target of the rebel action. They've threatened to kill him, not to mention the other students, if Fahzal does not publicly repudiate the Nationalist Party's agenda and then publicly step down. The crisis has been dragging on, with the terrorists periodically issuing demands. But, while the threat against Fahzal's son is in force, the government won't send anyone in to break the stalemate. The terrorists are dug in but good and there's no telling what defenses they've rigged on-site. The longer the standoff goes, the greater the chances that it will end with something deadly on a massive scale. Something's got to be done to break it."

"You know I don't like to see that kind of thing," Bolan acknowledged, "but I still don't see what our involvement is. It still sounds like something for the locals to work out for themselves."

"As I said, it *would* be," Brognola told him, "if not for Malaysia's somewhat delicate diplomatic involvement in Southeast Asia."

"And that is?" Bolan asked.

"For all its faults internally," Brognola said, "Fahzal's government has been a very strong one. Malaysia is doing well economically and, until now, the nation has been very stable. Malaysia's neighbors are anything but stable at the moment. Border tensions between Thailand and Cambodia are threatening to spill over into Burma and further destabilize that country, which is having its own problems getting along with its rival and neighbor, Bangladesh. Fahzal's government has extended feelers to both Burma and Bangladesh to see if it can help mediate the dispute, and they've been asked, not for the first time, to play diplomatic go-between for the Thais and Cambodians. As far as we can tell, it's working, too. Fahzal's diplomatic corps has managed to get all the parties to their respective tables for a series of premeeting confabs, ironing out the ground rules for the eventual peace talks."

"What does Fahzal get from all of that?" Bolan asked.

"It makes him look like a big wheel on the international scene," Brognola said. "If Malaysia can orchestrate a lessening of tensions among its neighbors, it can stabilize the entire area. That's good for its economy, good for Fahzal's reputation, good for the nation's status around the globe and good for Fahzal's chances of reelection. Plus he gets invited to all of the best UN parties."

"I can imagine," Bolan said without humor.

"There's a Chinese and Indian ethnic ghetto, of sorts, that has sprung up over the last year roughly equidistant from Petaling Jaya and Kuala Lumpur," Brognola said. "It's not pretty—conditions are terrible, and the residents have been deliberately herded there by pressure exerted through Fahzal's government and his internal security forces. Those forces are hired thugs who answer only to Fahzal and a control hierarchy loyal to him. They're colloquially referred to as the Padan Muka. I'm told it translates to something like, 'Serves you right.'"

"Charming," Bolan said.

"Fahzal has dispatched the Padan Muka to roust ethnic Chinese and Indian Malays throughout Kuala Lumpur and its satellite urban areas," Brognola said. "It's getting bad, and it's going to get worse. If Jawan bin Aswan Fahzal is not returned unharmed Fahzal and the Padan Muka are threatening to raze that ghetto. Specifically, they're going to firebomb it out of existence and murder everyone within it. Padan Muka forces and Malaysian firefighters are being stationed around the perimeter of the ghetto. Nobody's being let in or out."

"I think I see where you're going with this," Bolan said. "Fahzal and his government are the linchpin."

"Exactly right," Brognola said. "Bad as he is, the stability of Fahzal's government is vital to the stability of Southeast Asia. If Fahzal gives the order to kill those people, it's going to touch off an ethnic civil war in Malaysia. That could spread to the neighboring nations, but even if it doesn't, Malaysia's inability to mediate the border disputes between its neighbors will probably lead to Thailand, Cambodia, Burma and Bangladesh falling to each other's throats again. The entire region will destabilize, and I don't have to tell you that it could have a far-reaching impact for the rest of the world."

Bolan lowered his voice, to be certain the cabbie would not overhear—though this did not seem likely over the road noise, the howl of the cab's much-abused engine and the cabbie's own stream-of-consciousness swearing, intent as he was on earning his lavish tip. "So I just have to stop BR from destabilizing the country, rescue Fahzal's son so Fahzal won't commit mass murder and prop up a potentially genocidal regime because to do otherwise would lead to widespread economic and political unrest throughout the entire region."

"And you have to do it," Brognola said without missing a beat, "while dealing with Fahzal's people, who will be trying to kill you the whole time."

"And that is because?"

"The CIA has certain networks and assets in Malaysia," Brognola said. "One of them will act as your guide when you hit the ground. We believe we can trust him. But chances are that Fahzal's people know about him and will, by extension, know about you as soon as your plane hits the tarmac. We've got no official standing in Malaysia, Striker. They tolerate our involvement only grudgingly, and then only because Fahzal isn't quite ready to earn the enmity of the United States directly."

"Then he should stay out of my way," Bolan commented.

"The CIA's network in Malaysia is…porous…at best," Brognola said. "They'll know why you're there, and they won't give a damn that you're trying to help. Fahzal's out to prove his country can compete with the big boys. He won't want you there. We suspect he's got plenty to hide that he doesn't want us to know. We believe he's concerned about what a random element—you—might be able to uncover. He'll be looking to put you in an unmarked grave somewhere in the countryside just as fast as he can make and take you."

"The Man must know that it's going to get bloody, if that's the playing field," Bolan said. "I may have to work around Fahzal's government in order for the country to remain stable, but I'm not going to pull any punches if his people are trying to kill me."

"Nor should you," the big Fed said. "Make no mistake, Striker. We want you to do what you do. Just make sure at the end of the day that the country doesn't explode. Stop BR. Stop Fahzal without taking him down completely. I'll be working from here to handle the rest, behind the scenes. Just keep the peace, however you have to do it. That's the goal."

"All right, then, Hal," Bolan had said. "Just get me there."

"Your tickets will be waiting at the counter," Brognola said. "Good hunting, Striker."

And that had been that.

Now, Bolan was in another cab, a world away from the streets of New York, in the middle of a bustling city that was no less vibrant—and far more dangerous, for him.

"Mr. Cooper," Rosli said, breaking Bolan from his reverie, "I believe we have a problem."

"The two taxis following us?" Bolan asked. He had been watching through the side mirror. The two cars had been trailing them since they left the airport.

"Yes," Rosli said, grinning. "You do not disappoint me, Mr. Cooper. They are moving up."

The two trailing car increased their speed, suddenly, horns bleating to clear other traffic as the twin vehicles moved up on either side of Rosli's cab. Bolan glanced left, then right, and had just enough time to see the muzzles of the submachine guns poking from the open windows of the two cars.

"Break left, now!" Bolan ordered.

Rosli shot him a glance, not understanding.

Bolan reached out and grabbed the steering wheel.

As the cab's tires squealed in protest and the vehicle careened toward the fender of the leading enemy, the submachine gunners in the trailing cars opened up, spraying Rosli's cab with gunfire.

The crash was deafening.

2

The sound of rending metal and shattering glass was nothing the Executioner hadn't heard before. As Rosli's cab ground its nose into the side of the closest of the pursuing cars, Bolan kicked at his door savagely. It took three kicks to force the tortured passenger-side door open, but then he was hitting the pavement rolling as the two crippled vehicles shed their momentum, limped across the street and collided with the far-side curb. Bolan's .44 Magnum Desert Eagle was in his fist as he rounded on the wrecked enemy vehicle.

He caught sight of movement from inside the taxi and began triggering 240-grain hollow points into the passenger compartment. The heavy rounds tore through the vehicle with merciless efficiency, pulping the gunners who were struggling to bring their automatic weapons to bear.

Bolan advanced. As he neared the taxi, now a tomb, he heard Rosli shout.

"Cooper! Down!"

He hit the ground without hesitation. A burst of automatic fire burned the air where he had been standing. The second taxi was coming around for another pass,

the shooters inside spraying and praying as their driver
cut across traffic with reckless abandon.

The Executioner was only too aware of the civilian
traffic filling the busy city street. This was no place for
a firefight. They were near an alley, the space between
two large colonial-style buildings. He ran and reached
into the open passenger door, grabbed Rosli—who was
still behind the steering wheel crouched as low as he
could get—and dragged him by his shirt through the
opening, to the street.

"Back! Back!" Bolan shouted. Rosli got the idea fast
enough and, with his revolver in his fist, traded fire with
the drive-by gunners while Bolan dragged him into the
alley.

"It will not take them long to—"

"No, it won't," Bolan said, cutting the man off. He
was already holstering the Desert Eagle and drawing his
Beretta 93-R machine pistol. He slapped the 20-round
magazine to be sure of its fit and extended the weapon's
small forward grip, flicking the selector switch to three-
round burst.

Bolan brought the Beretta up. The gunners weren't
terribly smart. Their unsuccessful vehicular assault had
told him that much. The enemy cars had outnumbered
Rosli's taxi and were of at least equal power and weight.
It should have been a lot harder to defeat them than
it had been. The shooters inside the car had been too
slow on the mark, as well, or he'd never have been able
to stop them all before they could effectively return or
preempt his fire. He didn't know *who* the enemy was,
though Brognola's warning about the Padan Muka kept
rolling around in his brain. If these were the best Prime
Minister Fahzal could field for brownshirts, the Executioner wasn't very impressed so far.

He raised his mental estimation of them a moment later when the first of the gunners entered the alley, one high, one low, already shooting. He realized they were armed with mini-Uzis. The deadly automatic weapons spat tongues of flame in the relative shadow of the alley. The sound of the brass spilling onto the pavement was lost in the roar of the guns.

Pressing himself against the wall of the alley, Bolan gave Rosli a helpful shove to push the man against the opposite wall. Rosli was smart enough to crouch low and take careful aim with his revolver. He picked off one of the shooters as Bolan extended his right arm, back against the wall, and took aim at another of them, feeling the automatic gunfire whistle past his face mere inches from his flesh.

The Executioner triggered a tri-burst that stitched the second man center-of-mass. The gunner fell without a sound, dead before he hit the ground. Bolan began to back up, sliding along the wall, aware that his movement would give him away and that he would have to be ready for that.

Two more gunners ducked into the alley, first firing blindly around the corner with their Uzis, then following the guns and rounding the corner. Rosli fired but missed. Bolan caught one man in the face with a three-round burst, then tracked and shot the next man.

A grenade *pinged* off the far wall, thrown from the alley mouth, and bounced down the narrow space toward them.

Rosli was closer. He saw the grenade and, without hesitating, stepped forward and planted a firm toe-kick with impeccable accuracy. The grenade whipped back the way it came.

"Down!" Bolan ordered.

The grenade exploded in the alley mouth. Bolan counted to three, his ears ringing from the blast, and popped up with the Beretta 93-R in both hands.

He was concerned about shrapnel, about any civilians nearby who might have caught that grenade blast. He couldn't fault Rosli for his fast action; the man had saved their lives. Had Bolan been closer he would have tried to direct the grenade farther up the alley rather than toward the open street, but he would not criticize the CIA operative; there was no point in second-guessing life-or-death combat decisions made in the heat of battle, done and over.

He advanced on the alley mouth. The bodies of the shooters he and Rosli had already killed were splayed in gruesome wreckage, torn by the explosion. Bolan had seen enough carnage in his lengthy personal war that the sight did not unnerve him, but he would never truly be used to it. The Executioner simply did what he had to do, and took in measured stride the dead men he left in his wake—men who had tried to take his life, or the lives of good men, women and even children.

He saw the third car before its occupants saw him. The four men within carried more submachine guns, Uzis all. Bolan braced himself against one wall of the alley, leveling the Beretta and letting his eyes flick left, then right, to check the immediate area for civilians. The streets of Kuala Lumpur were densely traveled and much traffic still sped by, but he saw no pedestrians nearby. There were only the shooters, still unidentified.

Bolan figured they were agents of Fahzal's unfriendly government, determined to prevent an outside interest from interfering in the nation's affairs.

He tracked the first man, pressed the Beretta's trigger and rode out the muzzle rise as the three-round burst knocked the man to the pavement. The other three shooters scattered, spraying bullets in his direction. The soldier backed off, letting the mouth of the alley shield him. Slugs chipped the concrete and sprayed him with a fine, abrasive dust. He squinted against the grit, leaned and returned fire.

He knew the Beretta's 20-round magazine was starting to run low. He pulled in his elbow to cant the weapon, ripped the magazine free and slapped home a loaded spare from his messenger bag. The deadly snout of the weapon pushed forward once more as he extended his arms, ready for all comers.

The shooters repeated the suicidal charge the men before them had made, plunging into the alley with their guns blazing. They were firing wild, without a real idea of just where their target was, and that was the difference between them and the Executioner. Bolan didn't fire blindly. Crouching on one knee, he aimed carefully and put a three-round burst into the center of the leading shooter.

The Beretta jammed open.

Bolan did not hesitate. He simply let gravity take the now-useless machine pistol as he dropped the gun and went for the Desert Eagle, drawing the big .44 Magnum hand-cannon in one smooth, fluid motion. The triangular muzzle of the big gun bucked as he triggered a pair of heavy slugs, taking one man in the throat and the other in the chest.

The second man kept coming.

Bolan fired again, aiming for the head. At the same moment, the wounded shooter, a giant of a man, lowered his head and charged. The slug furrowed the would-be killer's scalp—and then he and Bolan collided.

Bolan pulled the Desert Eagle in against his side,

prepared to fire from retention, to shoot the big man off of him, as they hit the pavement and the breath was squeezed from his lungs. He triggered one blast, to no visible effect, and as he did so, he felt his attacker's arms encircle his chest. The seemingly implacable foe began to crush the life from him.

Bolan tried to shoot again, but something had jammed the Desert Eagle's action, most likely his clothing with the gun pressed against his body. He was able to get his gun arm free and started beating the man in the head with the .44 Magnum pistol, clubbing him in the skull with all his strength.

There were shots. Though the growing gray haze encroached on his vision, Bolan registered the sound of shots. He began to feel himself losing consciousness, and some part of him understood that he was still hitting his foe in the head with his jammed weapon.

The pressure was suddenly gone. The attacker's arms went slack, and Bolan drew in a deep, haggard breath. Then the body on top of him was rolled off and Rosli's face appeared in the center of his field of vision. He blinked past the floating spots of light.

"There are none left," Rosli said, offering a hand. "We must go, and go quickly. They will be here very soon."

"Who?"

"Royal Malaysian Police," Rosli explained. "Someone will have called them." He looked around, as if expecting witnesses to appear by magic in the alley. They wouldn't have to; there had been plenty of civilians on the street, and Bolan could hear screams as alarmed pedestrians came upon the carnage.

"Do you have any contacts in the police?" he asked.

"None, I am afraid," Rosli said as he shook his head. "Most are paid off by Fahzal's people, and those that are not are corrupt enough in other ways. We dare not be caught. It will be as if these—" he jerked his chin at the dead men littering the alley "—caught us and took us away. It would be to our deaths."

"Who are they?" Bolan asked.

"This one," Rosli answered, pointing with the revolver to one of the dead men. "I do not know the others, but this one I recognize. I have seen him often enough, where Fahzal's dirty work is to be done. I think he is a lieutenant of some kind." He pointed to the other men. All were dressed in civilian clothes—loose-fitting tunics and light slacks similar to Rosli's own. "Many times they wear the black-and-brown uniform. Not so now, but I recognize that one all the same. These men are Padan Muka, Fahzal's private army. I can but assume they were sent to kill me, and, of course, anyone with me."

The Executioner paused to scoop up the jammed Beretta, throwing it into his shoulder bag. He put the Desert Eagle in there, as well. He made as if to search the closest of the dead men.

"There is no time," Rosli urged, grabbing his shoulder. "Come." He released Bolan's arm and they started walking quickly.

"There is little we can do in Malaysia without the government knowing. There are many spies within our ranks. I trust a few, but not many. Too many of those I don't are well aware of everything that occurs within the intelligence network here," Bolan's contact said.

They were moving swiftly to the opposite end of the alley, and Bolan could hear the distinctive horns of what could only be police vehicles approaching in the distance. Rosli tucked away his revolver, arranging his shirt to cover the weapon in his waistband.

"I've got to get to the school," Bolan said. "We're already burning time those kids don't have."

"I know," Rosli agreed and nodded. "It is not much farther. We go."

They emerged at the opposite end of the alley. The police sirens were growing louder, echoing after them. Rosli went to a line of small cars parked nearby and, without hesitation, smashed the window of the nearest one with the butt of his revolver. He reached in, hit the door locks and beckoned for Bolan to join him. The soldier slid into the passenger seat.

Rosli wasted no words. He hammered the steering-column collar loose and began muttering to himself as he reached inside with both hands. The engine began to stutter and then finally caught. Rosli shook one hand absently as if he had been cut or shocked. He hit the accelerator and pushed them out into the traffic that was moving past. It had seemed to Bolan that no one passing by had given them a second glance as the CIA operative stole the car in broad daylight.

"They will be calling the police," Rosli said, as if reading his mind. "But they would not risk confronting us directly. Why do you think I used the gun? People are not anxious to be heroes here, Mr. Cooper, but neither do they tolerate wanton crime. We will not be able to use this car for long. The police will be given the license plate and description, I have no doubt. It does not matter. We need not go far."

Bolan nodded.

As Rosli drove, Bolan opened the messenger bag over his shoulder and removed the Desert Eagle. The slide had not gone fully into battery; a round was half in and half out of the chamber. He yanked the big magazine, shucked the unfired round and put the loose round in his pocket, not trusting that it might not be deformed in some way. He racked the slide a few times, making sure nothing was amiss. Then he inserted a fresh magazine and chambered a cartridge before holstering the big pistol.

He was more concerned about the Beretta. There had been no time to get a package to him before he reached the school. Brognola had transmitted to his secure satellite phone several files breaking down the details of the operation, which Bolan had read on the flight to Kuala Lumpur. In those files, he had noted that a care package full of special toys from Stony Man Farm was on its way.

If things went down as they should, it wouldn't matter for the incursion at the school. The action would be long over before the Farm's courier reached Bolan in Malaysia.

The slide of the Beretta was jammed. He removed the magazine and discovered that the feed lips were bent, something he hadn't noticed in the very brief time he'd had to inspect the gear. He tested the top round in the magazine while he was looking, and decided that the spring felt weak, too. He dropped the magazine to the floor of the car. His prints weren't on file anywhere, and the weapons Rosli had provided would not be traceable to any operation run by the Farm; if some overzealous Royal Malaysian Police officer decided to claim the magazine as evidence, he was free to do so and feel good about himself.

He quickly removed the slide of the 93-R. This was harder to do than normal because Rosli was sliding in and out of traffic like a man possessed. The smell of abused brake pads filled the compact car's cabin and the engine screamed in protest.

He'd been able to travel with a small tactical flashlight. He took it from the pocket of his cargo pants and used its bright beam to illuminate the barrel and chamber from the muzzle end of the weapon. All seemed to be in order. He was intimately familiar with how the machine pistol should look and operate when properly functional. The finish had been badly scuffed by impact with the pavement, but nothing seemed damaged.

He reassembled the weapon, worked the slide a few times and, satisfied, started checking magazines. When he checked the spring tension and the feed lips of all of them, carefully, he inserted one and chambered the first round, setting the weapon's safety and holstering it in his shoulder rig.

"It is my fault," Rosli said. "I obtained the weaponry specified at your request. I should have been more meticulous."

"It happens," the Executioner said. "If gear has flaws, combat exposes them, without fail. And at the worst possible time."

"Yes, this is true. Your philosophy is wise."

"Not mine," Bolan said. "Murphy's Law."

"Just so. You are ready?"

"Yeah," Bolan said. "How long?"

"Now," Rosli said. "We are here."

Rosli guided the little car to a halt a block away from where the action was, from what the soldier could see. The two men stepped out of the vehicle.

"Where will you be?" Bolan asked Rosli.

"I thought I would be coming with you."

"No," Bolan said, shaking his head. "I work alone for

this part. Stay out of sight, but stay close. I may need what or who you know before this is over."

Without another word, the Executioner strode forward, toward the danger.

3

The school reflected the fact that it catered to the progeny of the wealthy and powerful. The building was an impressive neocolonial structure, four stories, with an elaborate entranceway and a sizable property around it—especially by the standards of a densely packed city like Kuala Lumpur. A parking lot, with a ramp leading to further underground parking, was located at the west side of the building. The cars parked in it were almost all very expensive.

Uniformed Royal Malaysian Police had set up a cordon half a block from the school. From what Bolan could see, coupled with the intelligence data Brognola had provided, every road leading to the school was blocked off. Wooden barricades had been erected and there were plenty of weapons in evidence, mostly Kalashnikov rifles. The intelligence files had included the fact that Fahzal's regime was a regular purchaser of the Russian surplus arms, and that the first thing the Nationalist Party had done after sweeping to power was to authorize heavy expenditures upgrading or simply multiplying the weaponry used by both the military and law enforcement in the nation.

Fahzal's internal security thugs would be among those so armed, though apparently the prime minister's tastes ran to Israeli submachine guns as much as to Russian assault rifles. Bolan saw several knots of men in brown-and-black uniforms that could only be Padan Muka, based on what Rosli had told him. They had the dull, contemptuous look that he associated with goons of that type—people who enjoyed hurting others and who didn't do much thinking about that, or anything. They weren't soldiers and they certainly weren't patriots, not in the righteous sense; they were hired muscle, and they were predators. The nearest Padan Muka triggermen eyed him hard as he passed them, giving him a cold look.

He'd dealt with their kind before, and taught more than a few of them very painful lessons. There was no time to indulge his sense of justice on nonpriority targets, however.

Brognola's slim dossier had included the layout of the building he was now encountering. On the plane, he had formulated the most basic of plans, which left a lot to chance. He'd made his earliest incursions in his war against society's predators perfecting his abilities at role camouflage, and what he was about to do was an aspect of that. Fixing his gaze on a point far ahead of him, he looked past everyone who noticed him, as if he were irritated, rushed and focused on getting to some point beyond each of the glaring Padan Muka fighters and police officers. He got past the first set of barriers simply by acting as if he belonged there.

He was counting on complacency. The barricade of the school, and the hostage crisis within, was in its second day. The guards outside, perhaps expecting fireworks early on, would have had plenty of reasons to get bored by this time. They'd have gone from expecting anything to expecting nothing; the human mind sought routine and pattern even when there was no rational reason to expect either.

More significantly, they'd be expecting either violent enemy action or deadly subterfuge. They were focused on the school and on stopping that enemy action from within. They would not be expecting an incursion from outside, nor would they automatically think they should prevent someone outside from going in. After all, how crazy would a man have to be to want to enter a building held by dangerous, armed terrorists willing to threaten the lives of children?

The hard part, therefore, was not getting past the cordon outside the school. As the Executioner nodded and brushed past the barricades, brazenly walking through them as if he belonged there, nobody challenged him directly. He had known it would probably work, but in the back of his mind he had been prepared to shoot his way through if necessary. There was no time to do otherwise, and no viable alternative.

When he reached the front doors of the school, a few of the Royal Malaysian Police officers began to shout at him. It was possible they hadn't thought he'd do something so direct; perhaps they'd assumed he was simply moving toward the foremost barriers. Whatever they were shouting, he couldn't understand it, anyway. He figured they probably wouldn't shoot him for fear of touching off something inside the school.

Probably.

There were three sets of double doors within the front entrance. Each door was heavy, polished wood with brass fittings. The fogged glass of the doors has been starred with bullet holes, probably during the initial stage of the BR capture of the building. Bolan simply put his hand out and, ignoring the shouted protests from the men at the barricades, threw the doors open and stepped inside.

There were two men dressed in camouflage fatigues standing inside the doorway. They turned as he entered, but were apparently too baffled by his sudden appearance even to bother shooting him. They both held well-worn Kalashnikov clones, which they pointed at him.

"Hello there," Bolan said cheerfully. "Do either of you speak English?"

The door slid shut on well-oiled hinges behind him. The click of the mechanism engaging echoed through the suddenly very quiet hallway.

The two BR men turned to look at each other, their expressions almost comical. They looked back at Bolan.

"I do," the one on Bolan's left said. "Who are you? How did you get in here?" His accent was heavy, but his English was excellent. He punctuated his words by jabbing the muzzle of his rifle at Bolan.

"Door was open," Bolan answered, shrugging. "I'm the negotiator," he said.

"Negotiator?"

"I was sent to hear your demands, make arrangements for their fulfillment," Bolan said. "What, they didn't tell you?"

The two men glanced at each other again, then back to Bolan. "You two are with the group called the, uh, the BR, right? Fighting for freedom for your oppressed ethnic group?"

"We fight the oppression of Fahzal!" the English speaker said proudly. His companion either knew enough English to agree, or recognized the tone; he smiled and nodded with equal pride.

"Yes, by threatening to kill children," Bolan said. "But thanks. It would have been irresponsible of me not to check."

As he said the words, Bolan knew both men's brains would be focused on the dialogue he had created with them, and not immediately on his actions. They had already, thanks to his assertion, formed an opinion in their minds as to his purpose there.

The six-inch blade of the stiletto snapped open in his hand. He swung the knife up and slashed out across both of their throats in turn. Bolan sidestepped to his right, his right hand completing the arc. He elbowed the closest man in the back of the head to drive him to the floor. The other terrorist, the man who had spoken, fell to his knees clutching at his throat. He died with his eyes wide, trying and failing to say something with his last breath.

Bolan bent, picked up the better-looking of the two assault rifles and checked it. He grabbed the spare magazines the terrorists had carried, then took a moment to pop open the second rifle, pull the bolt and drop that bolt into his bag. There was no point in leaving functioning weapons behind him if he could help it.

It was time to get down to business, before those two were missed.

Neither man appeared to have a wireless phone or a walkie-talkie. That meant that either the terrorists were operating according to a preset plan, or they were using runners to transmit messages to the different teams securing the building. Either way, Bolan had just opened a gaping hole in their perimeter at the school's front door. He had to make sure they were too busy with him to realize that fact. And he'd have to hope that the forces outside didn't discover it, blunder in and make everything a lot more complicated. They were already going to be agitated, knowing that an unknown quantity had waltzed right past their roadblocks.

He considered the situation as he assessed his immediate environment for more threats. Brognola's briefing had included some notes on the political climate surrounding the events of the past day and a half in Kuala Lumpur. Ostensibly, Fahzal's government wasn't mounting a counterterrorist operation to retake the school for fear of what would happen to Fahzal's son, Jawan, and to the other hostages. Realistically, if Fahzal was the sort of man who was willing to use his son's kidnapping as an excuse to carry out a genocide, it wouldn't be out of the question that he might be prolonging the episode deliberately. Every moment of bad press the BR got was a nail in the coffin of both that group and the Chinese-Indian ghetto between Kuala Lumpur and Petaling Jaya.

Bolan knew it was a standard policy of such regimes. First, you used a common enemy to generate support for your cause, even if that enemy was contrived. Then, you herded all of your supposed enemies into a centralized location, where you could control and monitor them. And finally, you solved the contrived problem by killing the enemies you'd rounded up.

Bolan couldn't help but think that was the real motive here. Fahzal may not have anticipated his own boy being caught in the cross fire, but the soldier figured the Malaysian prime minister would have found another excuse to raze the ghetto if this one hadn't come up. If the BR's brutal activities could be used to paint all of the members of that ghetto neighborhood with the label of child-killing terrorists, it was likely Fahzal would be able to justify his actions with at least some of the international community. He most certainly would be able to use it as an excuse, a rationale, for his brutal tactics at home.

The Executioner didn't intend to let him get that far.

The foyer, opening up from the double doors, had a small door set at the far end. Bolan cautiously checked this and found a storage closet with a floor buffer inside. He dragged the two bodies into the closet, throwing the now useless Kalashnikov in after them. He paused a moment, then placed the functional Kalashnikov with its magazines in a corner of the storage room, under the mop and bucket standing next to the buffer. Much as the firepower might be needed, he could not risk going full-auto, and he needed to be able to travel fast and light. He eased the door shut. Then he paused and simply listened.

It was eerily quiet inside. He could hear voices amplified through bullhorns outside, probably the police or Padan Muka throwing demands at the terrorists or at the Westerner who had just blundered into their midst. Given that Fahzal's people, or at least those at the upper levels, knew the CIA had brought in a troubleshooter they didn't want, the soldier was a little surprised no one had taken a shot at him at some point. Bureaucracy seemed to be working in his favor; even a despotic regime like Fahzal's had many tentacles, and the dozens or hundreds of right hands didn't know what the dozens or hundreds of left hands were doing at any given moment.

The sound of the bullhorns was faint through the heavy front doors. Even if they had no reason to want to shoot him on sight, Bolan knew that walking so boldly into the midst of this hostage crisis might prompt a reaction from the police and troops outside. He was, however, gambling hard that it wouldn't. He could smell politics here. He was going to bet his life that the armed men outside would stay right where they were until Fahzal was ready to move—and not before.

Bolan consulted the intelligence files in his secure satellite phone. On the small color screen he called up the floor plan of the building. It might or might not be completely accurate; the plans were those originally filed for the construction of the structure a few years before. Had those plans been altered during construction, or had the building been renovated subsequently, the information in the soldier's phone could be flawed. That did not matter. He would work with what he had. This was why Brognola and the Man had chosen him for a seat-of-the-pants, near-suicidal mission of this type. Bolan gave the Justice Department's Sensitive Operations Group plausible deniability if things got ugly. He could be dismissed as a rogue operative for whom the United States would claim no responsibility. Much more important, he was the type of flexible, veteran combat operative who could roll with a fluid situation and come out on top, trusting his guts, his guns and his sense of intuition to get the job done.

According to the floor plan, the classrooms were located on the second and third floors. The main floor was used for administrative facilities and consisted of small offices. The fourth floor boasted a large auditorium with skylights and roof access.

Bolan put himself in the position of Fahzal's forces. That roof would almost certainly be covered by snipers, and unless the skylights could be blocked somehow, there would be a clear line of sight to anyone in the auditorium. That would mean the BR terrorists wouldn't set up in the auditorium, despite the convenience of having a large, open space to keep their hostages corralled. That is, they wouldn't set up in the auditorium unless they were profoundly stupid. Bolan had no reason to think they would be.

He was left, then, with the classrooms on the middle two floors, and that would make things more difficult. He would have to search room by room, eliminating resistance as we he went, doing it as quietly as he could to avoid alerting the others. The closer he got to the BR troops and their hostages, the more danger there was that he could tip off all of them to his presence. To succeed, he had to retain the element of surprise, but each guard, each terrorist he eliminated along the way, increased the odds of his detection.

Attaching the sound-suppressor to the Beretta 93-R, he made a cursory, hurried sweep of the ground floor, moving quietly heel-and-toe with the weapon held in both hands before him.

There was, according to the plans, another ground-floor entrance ahead and to the right, at the side of the building. Bolan made his way to the middle of the hallway, his civilian hiking boots quiet enough on the polished marble floor. Some part of his brain took note of the extensively carved moldings and ceiling art that decorated the interior of the school. No expense had been spared. The elaborately worked and padded benches that occasionally dotted the walls, outside of the administration offices, appeared to be very expensive, too, though Bolan was no expert on furniture.

He found the access hallway to the side entrance, opposite the metal doors of an elevator that he ignored.

Approaching the access hallway, he risked a glance around the corner. There was a fatigue-clad man standing there with his back to Bolan. The Executioner thought it odd that the noise of his conversation with the guards at the front entrance had not brought this one to investigate. Then he heard the tinny sound of music, coming faintly from the guard's head.

The man was wearing a portable music player. An AK-47 was slung over his shoulder. While he did seem intent on the view through the windows set on either side of the doorway, as if expecting a police raid at any moment, he certainly wasn't *listening* for trouble.

Wondering if this really was amateur night after all, Bolan raised his Beretta and pointed the sound-suppressor at the back of the sentry's head.

"Hey," he said softly, as he nudged the man with the barrel.

The sentry's head whipped around. He gasped, sucked in a breath to scream and grabbed for his rifle.

Bolan put a single round quietly through the man's face. The terrorist folded in on himself and was still.

That was another hole in the perimeter security. Bolan could hear the ticking of the clock deep in his mind, constantly aware of the mission's time constraints.

He kept going, finishing his sweep, quickly checking for stragglers or hidden shooters among the offices. As he neared the door at the far end of the corridor, which led to the stairwell, he caught a glimpse of movement through the small reinforced glass window set within the fire door.

He crouched low and pressed himself against the wall next to the door. The heavy door prevented him from hearing whomever was on the other side, but it could only be a sentry. Transferring the machine pistol to his left hand, he used the knuckles of his right to rap on the metal door. He knocked quietly but insistently.

The dark-skinned man who pushed the door open was wearing camouflage fatigues and aiming a Makarov pistol. Bolan fired, putting a single 9-mm round through the man's head. He dropped like a stone.

The Executioner scooped up the Makarov and tucked it into his belt behind his left hip. He had to move; there was no time to worry about the sentry's body. He had to keep up his pace in order to take the second, then the third floors.

Things had already gotten bloody. They were, he knew, about to get much, much worse.

4

Bolan crept up to the second floor and cautiously opened the fire door leading to the corridor beyond. There was no one waiting. The hallway was as impressive as the ground floor in its furnishings and decoration, but there were subtle differences. Bulletin boards lined the walls, and artwork obviously made by the students was on display. Brognola's files had said the school catered to children aged roughly seven to twelve; Fahzal's boy Jawan was twelve years old. The art on the walls was the usual fare produced by children in that age range the world over. Seeing it there, and knowing that BR was threatening those children with death, brought a hard gleam to the Executioner's eyes. He'd seen far too many innocents caught in the cross fire of power plays like these.

He began working his way down the hall. The layout was simple: there were half a dozen classrooms on each side, spaced exactly opposite each other, with more of the benches he had seen downstairs to break up the monotony. At the center of the hallway was an elevator on one side and a pair of doors leading to the boys' and girls' bathrooms opposite that.

He checked each classroom in turn. Each was empty. Satisfied that the second floor was all but deserted, he went back to the stairwell.

On the third floor, there were two guards waiting in the hallway. They were Indian Malaysians, from the look of them, and they wore the same camouflage uniforms Bolan had seen on the BR terrorists to this point. Both men had assault rifles. They were engaged in a heated conversation that Bolan could just barely hear from his side of the fire door. It sounded like Manglish, the curious version of English that the locals spoke.

One of the men turned and apparently caught a glimpse of Bolan peering out through the small reinforced window of the fire door.

Bolan didn't hesitate. As their weapons came up, he was already throwing open the door. The two were close enough that the heavy metal door slammed into the first of the pair, knocking him into his partner and sending them both sprawling. Bolan stomped, hard, pinning one of them to the floor with a heel to his groin. The man doubled over, still clutching his rifle.

The other sentry was recovering and the muzzle of his weapon was tracking up to Bolan as if in slow motion.

The Executioner was faster. The sound-suppressed Beretta clapped once, punching a single slug through the center of the man's forehead. He fell back and was still. Bolan turned his weapon on the other sentry, who was looking up at him in wild-eyed terror mixed with pain.

Bolan put his finger to his lips, gesturing for quiet.

A snarl of defiance was the sentry's response. He jerked his rifle, ready to fire from his back.

Bolan's Beretta silenced him forever.

He left the bodies. He repeated the sweep pattern he

used on the floor below, checking each room in turn, expecting at any moment to find a huddled group of students surrounded by armed BR thugs.

He found nothing.

Once again he checked each room directly, looking for anyone who might be hidden. There was no one. That meant that, in defiance of any logical, rational tactical analysis, the students would be on the fourth floor, almost certainly in the auditorium that dominated that floor. But why? It made no sense.

Bolan reentered the stairwell, careful to check for trip wires or other booby traps. Something wasn't right.

He emerged from the stairs to the fourth floor. The corridor there was wide and included an outlet for the elevator. Ahead of him, the doors to the auditorium waited. They were stained wood, very tall, with the most elaborate carvings he'd yet seen in this ornate building.

There were no guards. Bolan moved quietly to the doorway, performing a tactical magazine change in the Beretta, dropping the partial in an outer pocket of his messenger bag and inserting a fresh one. There was a very slight gap between the two doors. Mindful that he would be visible from the other side as a sudden shadow if he were at all back-lit, he peered through the gap with one eye, the Beretta held low against his body.

What he saw explained a great deal, and made the situation that much more complicated.

The BR terrorists were indeed gathered in the auditorium. He couldn't see the skylights from his vantage point, but he now understood why Fahzal's men weren't using snipers to shoot the killers inside.

What looked like a dozen adults—probably the school's faculty and support staff, anyone who was

caught in the building when the BR took control—
were grouped in a section of the auditorium seating
at the center of the room. On the stage, maybe forty
students representing every age range of the school's
student body were seated cross-legged on the polished
wooden platform. There were plenty of students and
teachers not accounted for, because the BR had—again,
according to Brognola's files—hit the school early in
the morning, before everyone was scheduled to arrive.
It made good tactical sense; they had plenty of hostages
and had nabbed Jawan, their primary target, but didn't
have scores of extraneous students and teachers getting
in their way.

The BR terrorists moved up and down the aisles,
walking off nervous energy, or they loitered about in
what were probably assigned sections of the auditorium.
Bolan counted at least ten of them, though he knew there
might be more he couldn't see from where he stood.

Several of the BR terrorists wore devices strapped to
their chests.

Too small to be suicide bombs, the packages on each
man's chest were just large enough to be transmitters.
Bolan eased his secure satellite phone out of his pocket,
positioned the lens of the camera built into the phone
and snapped a silent photograph of one of the men. He
transmitted the image to Stony Man Farm with a single
line of text: *Urgent, ID*.

What concerned Bolan more than anything, and what
made the devices on the terrorists' chests so important,
was that several of the huddled faculty members wore
what looked like explosive belts.

He did not have to wait long. His phone began to
vibrate quietly and he hit the answer button, placing the
phone to his ear.

"Striker, this is Price," Barbara Price said without waiting for him to speak. Stony Man Farm's honey-blonde, model-beautiful mission controller would be fully aware of just what Bolan was doing, and she would know he was not necessarily free to speak aloud. "I'm transferring you to Akira now." The voice of Akira Tokaido, the Farm's resident electronics and computer genius, came on the line.

"Striker, Akira," he said. He, too, knew not to waste time, or expect an answer verbally. "I enhanced the image you sent us and I believe I have an identification. Those are Iranian-made dead-man's switches. They're designed to monitor heartbeat. It is very likely that if one of those men is killed, his transmitter will activate. Effective range is not far, perhaps fifty yards. Are there explosives nearby? If so, they are very likely to be rigged to those transmitters. One other thing—that particular model is very primitive. It is not fail-safe. It can be jammed easily enough, and if it is damaged, it does not transmit. In its normal state it is off, unlike some suicide switches that transmit until the wearer dies or the mechanism is damaged, with the signal loss being the trigger."

Price came back on the line. "That's all there is, Striker. We stand ready to assist you."

Bolan mashed the keys and sent a quick string of text gibberish by way of acknowledgment; Price and the team at the Farm would know what he meant. He closed the connection and put his phone away.

Well, that was that, then. Obviously the terrorists had informed Fahzal's government of just what would happen if any of their people in the auditorium died. No doubt the transmitters were connected to the explosive belts on the teachers. It was a particularly cowardly act, using innocent men and women as human shields, threatening to blow them apart if the BR came under attack.

Tokaido had obviously known what Bolan would have in mind, to have mentioned the vulnerability of the transmitters. He was hindered only by logistics. He was one man, facing many, and he would have to be very, very precise. Fortunately for those trapped within, there were very few men more skilled with a firearm than Mack Bolan.

This would not be the first time he had done something of this type, testing his marksmanship against multiple targets that required exact placement of his shots. There were far more targets this time, though. Those targets might be in motion and shooting back at him the entire time, and some might be hidden. He would need to identify the transmitter-wearing terrorists while in the heat of battle, and he would have to be very careful to miss none of them.

What he was about to do would require all of his skill and all of his concentration. He would have to rely on years of experience assessing threats, identifying and differentiating targets. He would need every ounce of ability he possessed in terms of his reflexes, his speed, his resolve.

He was ready.

Bolan removed the suppressor from the 93-R. He did not need the added factor of firing through the device, which could cause shots to angle in unpredictable ways. As it was, he knew this particular Beretta fired high low and left; he could compensate for that. Flicking the weapon's selector to single shot, he drew the Desert Eagle and made sure it was cocked, safety off.

He placed his fingers against the door and tested it.

It gave slightly; it wasn't locked. He backed up, braced himself and drew a deep breath.

His foot pistoned forward and he smashed the door inward with a powerful front kick.

The Executioner threw himself into the auditorium, already picking his targets. He fired the Beretta in his right hand. The slug punched through the transmitter of the nearest terrorist, boring through the device and the heart of the man who wore it.

With his left hand he pressed the trigger of the Desert Eagle, tracking a different terrorist. He fired the big hand-cannon, and the .44 Magnum slug blew the transmitter apart as it punched a massive exit would out the man's back.

The Executioner killed another terrorist, and another. He moved through the auditorium like the scythe of the Grim Reaper, both weapons firing simultaneously, dropping terrorists in two directions at once.

The answering fire tore up the seats of the auditorium. The terrorists may or may not have expected police action, but they had probably thought to see it coming; a massive counterterror operation would have tipped off the guards on the lower floors. They were not prepared for a lone gunman, a highly motivated and experienced fighter who moved among them like a shark moves among a school of fish. Individually and as the BR, they probably thought of themselves as dangerous men. In the presence of the Executioner, they were like brutal children, only slightly less helpless in the face of Bolan's righteous fury than were the innocent civilians they had taken hostage.

He was constantly in motion. He moved as quickly as he could while still maintaining a stable, fluid firing platform, acquiring targets and dealing death to the terrorists with calm, cool accuracy. Several wild blasts of automatic fire tore up the floor around him and the furnishings near him, but it was as if Bolan did not even see it. He ignored the hail of fire, ignored the shouts of the BR men, ignored the muzzle flashes and the ringing of ejecting, empty brass and the deafening sound of his and their guns.

One of the BR men, perhaps desperate, perhaps simply vengeful, turned his weapon on the stage. The angle was all wrong, and Bolan couldn't get the chest shot he needed. Extending his arm, still moving and firing the Beretta 93-R, he tapped a .44 Magnum round from the Desert Eagle into the terrorist's shoulder. The impact spun him toward Bolan—and the Executioner punched a second .44 Magnum slug through the center of the device strapped to the BR shooter's chest.

Another terrorist brought up a revolver and aimed it at the crowd of bomb-strapped adults. Bolan spared him a single 9-mm round through the face, as he was one of several men not wearing a dead-man's switch.

Bolan felt a slug sear past his abdomen and another take a chunk from his calf. He stumbled, but did not falter. His guns tracked the sources of both rounds and he dropped two more would-be killers.

As he moved, as he fought, as he fired both guns dry, the Executioner never stopped seeking the critical targets—the transmitters strapped to the chests of the BR gunmen. He let the Desert Eagle fall from his hand. There was no way to reload it, not with only one hand. Then he reloaded the 93-R with a fresh magazine, moving as fast as he had ever moved in his life in the heat of battle. He shot another man, and another, and fired a round through the center of yet another dead-man's switch.

Suddenly, it was over.

Bolan's ears were ringing so badly that he didn't notice the first of the heavy rounds from above. The back of an auditorium chair exploded in a burst of stuffing, wood splinters and red upholstery.

Snipers.

The gunfight had been too much for the police to maintain their fire discipline; they'd either started shooting on their own, or the order had been given. Bolan dived clear and rolled into the shelter of one of the rows of seats, where he couldn't be seen from the skylights. There were a few more shots, but eventually they ended. Bolan knew that, given the lighting outside versus in the relatively dim auditorium, any shots the snipers took were essentially half-blind. That was why they hadn't managed to take his head off. The hostages were just lucky none of them had been killed.

Bolan knew he really didn't have much time. The police outside would be entering the building and securing it floor by floor. He spotted the Desert Eagle, crawled over to it and picked it up. He reloaded it and the Beretta once more.

"Is everyone here okay?" he shouted. "Is anybody hurt?"

There was a pause. Finally, one of the adults said in perfect English, "Yes, sir! We're okay here, sir. The children are shaken but none of them have been harmed."

"Who am I talking to?" Bolan yelled back, still hidden by the seats.

"Steve Barone, sir. I teach English."

"American?" Bolan asked.

"Yes, sir. You, too, sir?"

"Yes," Bolan said. "Listen, Barone, I can't explain, but things are about to get very difficult for me. I'm not wanted here, and the authorities are going to kill me if they can identify me."

"I...I think I understand, sir."

"Cooper. Call me Cooper."

"Cooper," Barone said.

"Barone, is Jawan, the prime minister's son, all right? He's not hurt, is he?"

"He's not here," Barone said. "They separated him very early on, almost from the first moments of the attack on the school. I think they took him somewhere, sir. I don't know where. We haven't seen him since."

"That's a problem," Bolan said. "Did you overhear anything? Did any of them say anything that might indicate where he's being held?"

"I'm afraid not, Mr. Cooper. Uh...sir? These explosives..."

Bolan crawled his way over to where the teachers were huddled. He had no trouble spotting Steve Barone, who was looking right at him as he approached. The man was clearly a Westerner, blond, blue-eyed, a good head taller than most of the other faculty. He was still wearing the explosive vest the terrorists had fitted him with.

"They're going to be here soon," Bolan said. "Let me check that quickly." He looked over the harness but found no hidden trips or switches, no wires connected to the buckles. The terrorists had simply strapped the belts on and then tied the prisoners' hands.

Bolan used his knife to cut the ropes binding Barone's wrists. "Can you manage with the others using just your hands?" he asked.

"I can, Mr. Cooper," Barone said, nodding eagerly. He took the vest off, carefully. "Uh..." He placed the harness with its explosive belts gently on the floor. "Can these still go off?"

"Unlikely," Bolan said. "The detonators are all destroyed. They should be pretty stable or they'd have gone off by now. You're going to have to manage on your own, Barone. I've got to find a way out of here."

"They'll kill you, you said. They've got to be everywhere by now, and coming here," Barone said hesitantly. "If you'll…if you'll allow me? Sir, it isn't right, you giving your life to save us. I don't know who you are or who you work for, but I'll be damned if I'll let the man who saved all our lives sacrifice himself. I don't know *why* you say the police want to hurt you, but…how do you feel about English?"

"Come again?"

"Teaching English, Mr. Cooper. How would you feel about joining our staff?"

5

The sprawling ethnic ghetto squatting between the out-skirts of Petaling Jaya, extending north and east toward Kuala Lumpur, was an affront to Nasir's senses. The gaunt, almost skeletal man, his head shaved bald, wore the black-and-brown uniform of the Padan Muka. The epaulets on his uniform shirt bore testimony to his rank within what some uncharitably called Malaysia's secret police. The gold bars that declared him unquestioned leader of the security forces at Fahzal's command.

Nasir Muzafar was feared by all of Malaysia. At least, those with any intelligence at all knew enough to be afraid. If he could not command the respect of all he encountered, Nasir knew he could at least command their terror.

Nasir's lip curled in disdain as he surveyed the cor-rugated metal and plywood huts, some covered with tarps and other makeshift barriers to the wind and rain, that were the direct result of Prime Minister Fahzal's policies.

Fahzal's policies were, of course, his own. Every man of great power had a more powerful man to direct him. The power behind the throne was a universal concept.

Nasir, as head of Fahzal's internal security forces, was naturally that power, and had staked it out for himself when the two of them were simply moving up within the machinery of the Nationalist Party.

Fahzal was far from a true believer, which did not bother Nasir. Fahzal had determination, and he had force of will. He could hold an audience and, more importantly, he could project strength. If that strength was not truly his own, what of it? It meant that a man who understood how to guide others to power could channel his own strength through such a vessel, improving a nation that wanted to be led.

Nasir and Fahzal were not founding members of the Nationalist Party. Nasir had joined the group in its infancy, recognizing the potential in its rallying cry of Malaysia for Malaysians. He had found and courted Fahzal politically when Fahzal was simply a low-level government functionary, sitting behind a desk in the department of public works. That had been a dreadful waste of potential, as Nasir saw it. He was familiar with everyone and everything in Malaysian government, of necessity, for he had long made the halls of power his territory. The rise to power of Fahzal was testament to Nasir's determination to improve their great land. Removing the nation's inferiors, purging Malaysia of the blight and drain on its fabric, was simply a necessary function, one the Nationalist Party chose to recognize explicitly.

Nasir knew that there were those who, foolishly or naively, considered him monstrous for what he advocated, for what he implemented. He didn't care. The halls of power were no place for the weak. Not the weak of heart, not the weak of mind and certainly not the weak of stomach. True power required a willingness to make hard decisions, to do what no one else was willing or able to do.

If Nasir had a talent, it was spotting abilities in others. Early on he had spotted the ability of Fahzal to lead, to galvanize, to motivate. Fahzal, reasonably pliable himself, had a streak of cold meanness in him that Nasir could appreciate. Nasir simply fed Fahzal the beliefs he thought most appropriate, reinforced those beliefs in conversation while stroking the man's ego, surrounded Fahzal with functionaries and admirers who further stated those beliefs. It was as if he were telling the prime minister what he believed, and why, so simply and easily.

Fahzal did have a certain zeal, once Nasir got him wound up and headed in the right direction. That was one of the things that made their partnership so ideal. And it *was* a partnership, for Nasir had no desire to be the man on the throne—and thus the man held responsible for both success and failure. No, he was quite content to work as he did, to lead the Padan Muka. Besides, running the internal security force was like being the general of his own army. Fahzal gave him the authority to direct the Padan Muka as he saw fit—but that idea was Nasir's to begin with, and thus Nasir wrote his own authority.

He stood, a pair of binoculars in his hands. An Uzi submachine gun was slung over his shoulder, across his body. He wore a pouch of extra loaded magazines for it, and in his belt was the curved *jambiya* knife he had carried every day of his adult life. Many men and no small number of women had ended their lives on the end of that blade. Nasir enjoyed looking into their eyes when that happened. He was fascinated by the subtle change, by the fading of the light behind the eyes that was the dividing line between life and death.

If asked, he would say that he took no pleasure in what he was forced to do for the good of his nation. At heart, Nasir knew that this was not strictly true. There was, he had long ago decided, no harm in enjoying his work. It made no difference in the ultimate disposition of his efforts, after all.

The security team flanking him was beginning to grow agitated. Majid had disappeared some thirty minutes earlier and had not yet returned. No doubt they were starting to fear that Nasir's most trusted field lieutenant, the man who answered to no one in the Padan Muka save for Nasir himself, was lost to the rebels. They could hear sporadic gunfire from within the ghetto. The shots were spaced very far apart and so they had been having no luck tracking the source.

Plumes of smoke rose from the ghetto, too, but the fires being set were small and had been kept deliberately so. The rebels were not stupid. They were not going to burn down the very warren they were trying to protect.

The media Fahzal controlled or bullied into submission had, so far, been true to Fahzal's orders. They had deliberately blurred the distinction between BR, the radical terrorist group, and the ethnic Indian and Chinese Malays who made up the population of this teeming cesspool. Most of them were not murderous terrorists; they were simply intractable rebels who thought to resist the will of Fahzal. In resisting Fahzal, they resisted Nasir, and this was foolish. But Nasir at least understood the will to self-preservation. Their stubbornness would not save them, but the head of the Padan Muka could not condemn anyone, no matter how inferior, for trying to live when death came calling. It was just that their efforts were doomed to failure.

So far, the taking of the school, the kidnapping of Fahzal's son, Jawan, and the press coverage of both was having the desired effect. The Malaysian people were becoming more and more hostile to the Indian and Chinese groups within Malaysia's population. There would be no sympathy for the denizens of the ghetto when the siege began.

From the beginning of the hostage "crisis," Fahzal had—at Nasir's urging—stationed the Padan Muka at all entrances and exits from the ghetto, making sure they had the troop strength, the weaponry and the support equipment they would need for an extended attack. Nasir had made sure his people knew that pressure was the goal. If they could strike fear into the people of the ghetto, they could push them to the breaking point, drive them crazy with terror. This would wear them down over time and make them that much less organized, that much easier to destroy utterly, when finally Fahzal declared publicly that his time limit had been reached and that those who had stolen his son would pay for their inhuman crimes.

Fahzal had hinted at an explicit deadline in the media, but he had not given one, and that was because Nasir had not given him one to pass on. Fahzal had asked about it, a few times, but Nasir had explained that the situation was very unsettled and thus no plans should be made until absolutely necessary. After all, once Fahzal's government announced a deadline, that deadline would have to be kept. They could not afford to look weak either domestically or on the international stage. And Nasir was having far too much fun in the meantime. He saw no reason not to indulge himself for a while longer, as all the while the hostage situation was garnering national attention and making the Indian and Chinese Malays look more villainous than ever.

Nasir knew that in politics, perception was reality. It would not matter, now or when histories were written, what had truly happened. It only mattered that Nasir be able to dictate what he said had happened. History was always written by the winners, and the winners were always the strong. Nasir understood strength most of all. He despised weakness in all forms.

That was the worst failing of the subraces he "persecuted," in their words. They were weak. They were a burden on the true Malaysians and the country those men and women had built. Too many of Nasir's pureblooded countrymen pitied the lesser races, the inferior nationalities. This was hopelessly naive. They were fortunate, even if they could not see it, that they had Nasir to do the hard things, the necessary things, the dirty things, that they could not do. They slept well in their beds because the rough men of the Padan Muka were willing to save them from themselves.

One of the security men said something Nasir did not catch, but his tone was understandable enough. The others were pointing, relieved, as they saw Majid emerge from the ghetto. He was leading a string of rebels, three men and two women, each handcuffed to the next.

Nasir had ordered Majid into the ghetto as a show of force, an object lesson for other Padan Muka officers who flanked him. He did not take lightly his responsibility to train, to forge, to build his men into the most effective security operatives he could make them. They would have to be able to do the difficult tasks with utmost efficiency and without hesitation, and thus he needed to be certain they were brutal enough and willing enough to get the job done.

Showing them what Majid could do, demonstrating that Nasir and Nasir alone held the leash of authority that kept Majid in check, was invaluable to their training. It was also a good idea to reinforce to those under him that Nasir's command was inviolable and total. If they knew that at the snap of his fingers, Nasir could send Majid alone into hopeless danger and expect him to return with prisoners beaten into submission, they would be that much less likely to challenge his authority. Those who did—though it was rare—either met their fate in Majid's hands when the big man crushed their skulls, or they met their ends at the tip of Nasir's *jambiya*.

Whenever possible, Nasir preferred to let his authority over Majid speak for itself. He enjoyed watching his lieutenant brutalize others, for in his way Majid was like an extension of Nasir's will. And Majid was enormous. While not the biggest man Nasir had ever met, he carried himself with the brute force of a gorilla. He was almost inhuman in that way. Dull of mind but ever loyal, he had the gait of a feral creature rather than a man. In his eyes, Nasir sometimes saw a flicker of what might have been intelligence, or of what might have been madness. It didn't matter at all, for Majid would always do as Nasir ordered, and had not deviated from that path in all the years Nasir had directed him.

Majid's loyalty was a function of gratitude. The big man had been toiling at hard labor in Malaysia's worst prison when Nasir, recruiting for the then-fledgling Padan Muka, had toured the facility looking for desperate men. Majid had recently murdered three other prisoners; the outlook for him was bleak. If the state did not execute him, certainly his fellow prisoners would conspire to murder him, and eventually they would succeed based on numbers alone. Majid therefore faced a death sentence no matter what he did, and as soon as he left solitary confinement, his days would be numbered. The big man was not terribly smart, but he understood that it was Nasir who had opened the doors of the prison and allowed him to walk out of it. What was more, Nasir had asked nothing of Majid except that the man continue to indulge his desires to hurt, to beat, to maim. The requests Nasir made of Majid filled the big, simple man with such joy that Nasir might have called it love, if he thought the hopelessly dim Majid were capable of any real emotion except the desire to inflict pain.

Before he found himself in prison, Majid had been a wrestler, courted by international mixed-martial-arts circuits as the Malaysian Monster. He had never been defeated in tournament competition, and might have gone on to become a star in the West's competitions if not for the fact that he had strangled his girlfriend. Nasir, perhaps in a brief moment of emotional weakness, had expressed curiosity about this just once. He had asked the big man, late one night as the two sat drinking in a bar in one of Kuala Lumpur's seedier districts, why he had done it. Had his woman offended him in some way? Cheated on him? Failed to please him?

Majid had simply shrugged. The expression on his face was almost completely blank. If he had a reason at the time, a *real* reason, it was apparently forgotten to him. The knowledge of this disturbed Nasir in some distant part of himself that was still not inured to pain, violence and death. He had vowed never to ask Majid anything like that again, and had done his best to forget it. Any emotion felt weak to him, and weakness had to be stamped out if great men were to accomplish great goals.

Majid carried a pistol in a holster at his side. The weapon was an ancient Smith & Wesson .44 Magnum revolver, so worn that the blue finish had completely rubbed off. The rusty gun still functioned reliably, but only because Majid dutifully cleaned it. He never used it except at Nasir's explicit orders. Majid preferred to kill with his bare hands. It was as if shooting an enemy never even occurred to him. When he wished to kill, he first sought to wrap his meaty hands around his victims before beating or squeezing the life out of them.

The big man stopped before Nasir with his string of prisoners, his expression full of innocent pride. He looked like nothing so much as a hunting dog delivering a recovered bird to its master.

"Rebels?" Nasir asked.

Majid nodded. "All," he said.

"Good." Nasir smiled. "The women are attractive enough. I see no reason they should not be put to good use." He pointed at them and then gestured to the Padan Muka officers present. They looked at each other, then to Nasir, then to the women and back again. "Well?" Nasir urged. "Do what you wish with them."

The women screamed. Majid cuffed one of them, which silenced the other one, too. He produced his handcuff key and unlocked the two females, who were dragged away by the other Padan Muka officers. The nearest metal huts would suffice, Nasir was sure, and it was not long before the women's cries became much more pained.

Nasir hoped the other rebels, not to mention the more cowed residents of the Indian and Chinese ghetto, would get word that this was happening. Nasir had ordered his troops to take advantage of opportunities for acts of brutality like this one, in order to increase the pressure on the ghetto's occupants. It did not hurt Nasir at all, either, because giving his men free rein to indulge themselves kept them happy. Happy foot soldiers were loyal foot soldiers, for the most part. They should know that loyal service to Nasir and to Fahzal had certain benefits, certain pleasures associated with it.

Nasir was not an ungenerous man, after all.

The women would be executed when his men were done with them. They would be of no use to anyone after, in any event. He thought perhaps he might take the time to stab one of them himself, simply to watch her eyes as the lights went out. He thought perhaps he owed himself that much. His only regret would likely be that, by the time he got to one of them, she would be too dazed to care, and might perhaps welcome the release of death. He did not like it at all when they hoped for death. Far better that they fight it, resist it, with all their strength. It was much more…fascinating…that way.

The three rebels left looked toward the hut, their hatred almost a living thing passing between them and Nasir. Nasir laughed at that. He nodded to Majid. "Start with that one," he said, pointing to the Indian among the group. The other two were Chinese.

Majid nodded. He advanced on the Indian, who was still cuffed to the other men. Wrapping his thick hands around the man's throat, he began to exert pressure. The rebel fell to his knees, clawing at Majid's hands and beating against the big man's chest, but Majid might have been carved of stone for all the effect this had.

The man's eyes were bulging in their sockets when Majid finally released him. The body fell hard, dragging the other prisoners down with it. They struggled against

the handcuffs that bound them, their terror driving them
to get away from this menacing figure who had so cal-
lously crushed the life from one of their friends.

Nasir suddenly had an idea. He pointed. "The one
on the end. Release him. Let him go back to his fellow
rebels and tell them what he has seen."

Majid nodded, unquestioning as always. He released
the handcuffs and gave the man a hard shove. The rebel
stumbled, but dragged himself back to his feet and ran.
Nasir laughed, thinking he had never seen someone
move so fast. It was as if an evil spirit were chasing the
poor bastard.

Perhaps it was, Nasir thought to himself. Perhaps, to
the inferior races and nationalities, men like Nasir and
his Padan Muka were akin to evil spirits. They were
only evil to those who were themselves wrong, Nasir
knew. But he knew he could not expect them to see it
that way.

He knelt before the remaining hostage and produced
the *jambiya*. Grabbing the man by the back of the head
with his free hand, he slipped the sharp blade in between
the man's ribs. The rebel looked at him with such total
shock and amazement that Nasir could not help but be
amused, and in his laughter he almost missed that rare,
wonderful moment when his prisoner gave up the last
of himself.

6

The underground cantina was thick with the smell of opiates, hazy with the smoke of cigarettes, pipes and hookahs. Mack Bolan and Rosli entered the cantina and waited just inside the door while their eyes adjusted. It was broad daylight outside, but dark as candlelit night in the bar.

Rosli had been looking at Bolan with something like disbelief ever since the Executioner had found him standing in the shelter of a doorway, a block from the liberated school. The two men found a table in one corner of the bar. Rosli ordered drinks for both of them, but he ordered in Malaysian, so Bolan did not bother asking. He assumed it would be something appropriate.

"I am sorry, Mr. Cooper." Rosli shook his head, smiling ruefully. "It is just that you simply walked in there. I would not believe it if I had not seen it. You just walked past the barricades and into the school."

"It's not really a big deal," Bolan said, shrugging. "There was a very good chance they wouldn't shoot me once they realized what I was doing, and I was counting on complacency to get me past the blockades in the first place."

"You gambled your death against that," Rosli said. "And you cannot discount just how odd a method it is for penetrating a terrorist stronghold, simply to open the front door and walk inside."

"It had the benefit of being unexpected," Bolan said.

"I am impressed, Mr. Cooper."

"Don't be," Bolan said. "Rosli, I didn't make some suicidal charge. I don't do what I do for personal glory or to prove what a man I am. I took a calculated risk in order to achieve a specific goal. A goal that still hasn't been reached. Are you going to tell me what we're doing here?"

"Yes, yes, of course, Mr. Cooper. My apologies. I did not mean to be cryptic. You told me that you needed to find your way up the chain of command of BR. This cantina, which exists somewhat outside of Malaysian police authority, is a known place of congregation for the BR's members. While Fahzal's government is strong, there are those places where its enemies hold sway. The police avoid this area, preferring to keep the BR contained to known areas of activity. They raid periodically, and when they do, the BR leadership knows to stay hidden. Now is one of those times, I suppose, given their bold operation at the school. The leaders would know to remain in hiding while their operatives drew such attention, forcing a crackdown. But there are always BR people in this area, no matter what. Some even persist during the police and Padan Muka raids, hoping to sell themselves dearly in order to die with honor and draw attention to the resistance. I guarantee that at least some of those here in this room, this very minute, have rebel sympathies. It is very likely some will have affiliation with the BR itself."

"You don't think we'd have better luck starting with, say, BR safe houses? Places where they're certain to be holed up?" the Executioner asked.

"You perhaps forget the somewhat unfortunate state of our intelligence network here," Rosli said, frowning. "I guarantee that any BR safe house my people know, the Padan Muka will know, as well. If they thought there was any chance you would go there, they would be waiting for us. They are probably watching the largest ones even now, on the off chance that I will be foolish enough to take you to one. No, Mr. Cooper, that is not the way. We must find our way to the BR through those in its ranks. We must have fresh intelligence, something Fahzal's government and his thugs do not yet know about."

"Fair enough." Bolan nodded. He was a soldier, not an intelligence operative, but he knew his way around well enough to recognize that Rosli spoke the truth. The man knew his craft, even as he knew just how compromised was the CIA's flimsy operation in Malaysia.

"You did not tell me how you managed to get out of the school after the police raided it," Rosli said.

"One of the faculty was an American-born English teacher," Bolan said. "He was grateful for our efforts to save him and the students. He's the one who told me BR took Jawan somewhere, when the attack first occurred."

"You say 'our efforts,'" Rosli chuckled. "You mean *your* efforts."

Bolan shrugged. "When the police investigated, they were looking for a tall, lone Westerner. They weren't looking for a couple of American English teachers among the faculty."

"So you…my gods, Cooper, you walked *out* just as you walked *in?*"

"Something like that."

"I shall have a story to tell my grandchildren, should I live to have them," Rosli said as he chuckled again.

The waiter, a wizened old Malaysian who looked to Bolan to be about a hundred years old, brought two steaming cups of Turkish coffee. Bolan raised an eyebrow.

"An unusual habit, I suppose." Rosli took his own cup and brought it to his lips, sipping the hot beverage delicately. "But one I cannot do without, and thought to share. Drink quickly, Mr. Cooper. I am known well enough to the BR, and thus you will be, too. We have already drawn attention."

"You knew this would happen?" Bolan asked.

"I thought it the fastest way. You approve?"

"I do," Bolan said. His hands were already beneath the table, as he scanned the room. "We need to move fast."

"Yes, of course," Rosli said. "There is none so fast as the hunted rabbit."

Bolan had nothing to say to that.

He was aware that there were three men at a table across the bar, eying them hard. One was Chinese and the other two appeared to be Indian. That in itself was nothing remarkable, but if this was a BR hangout, it was a telling indicator. When the men rose as one and approached Bolan and Rosli, the soldier braced himself for the confrontation that was about to begin.

The Chinese man said something in Malaysian to Rosli. The tone was hostile. Rosli said something back without looking up. Without changing his tone, he said quietly, "He is threatening to kill us. He says he knows

I am a spy of some sort. He says he will leave both our bodies in the alley behind this place."

"He does, does he?" Bolan said.

The Chinese man looked to Bolan, then back at Rosli—

Bolan struck. He lashed out with his knife still folded, using the closed knife like a pocket stick. The end of the heavy plastic handle slammed into the side of the Chinese man's head, just under his jaw, dropping him like a stone.

Bolan hooked his arm around the falling man and pushed him back, using him for leverage as he threw himself at the other two. He slammed the heel of his palm under the chin of the next man, then fired a horizontal elbow across the hapless man's face. Unconscious, the Indian crashed into his comrade, and Bolan shoved with all his might, knocking both men down. He pounced on the third man, kneeing him in the solar plexus, then stood and snapped open the blade of the knife.

He wasn't disappointed. He'd assumed the fight in the middle of the bar would draw the attention of any other locals loyal to these three. For that matter, just the idea of an outsider taking on Malaysians might draw resistance from the home team. The men who now approached, however, had the look of stone-cold killers. There were five of them, dressed in nondescript civilian clothes. All five were either dark-skinned Malays, or Malays of Indian descent. They held knives of their own.

Bolan was aware that Rosli had disappeared. He had gone somewhere during Bolan's charge; the soldier assumed his CIA guide knew how to take care of himself. It was just as well. He wouldn't want Rosli getting caught in the cross fire if things got really ugly, as they were about to.

"You're BR," the Executioner said, challenging.

The men hesitated. There was no immediate denial, and no confusion; only the reluctance to admit. It was slim, but good enough for Bolan. One of them spoke up, gesturing with his knife.

"You should not be here," he said, his accent thick but his English understandable. "We fight oppression. Do not interfere. Go while you can."

"Oppression?" Bolan asked. He squared off against the quintet, the knife low against his lead leg. "Does it fight oppression to strap bombs to innocent men and women? To fire an assault rifle into a crowd of children?"

"We are few and Fahzal's troops are many," the man said. "We must do everything we can to break his grip. Some will die. It is too bad that they must. But they must. Only if we are willing to do this will we be free."

"I understand fighting tyranny better than you think," Bolan told him. "But there's that, and there's terrorizing the innocent. You can't achieve the first by doing the second."

"You could have left," the man said. "Yes, we are BR. You will have to die now that you know that. But first you will tell us where that spy, Rosli, has gone."

"You know Rosli, do you?"

"He is well-known to us, yes," the BR thug said, nodding. "He is known to be a lackey to the West. He is not fit to be a Malaysian."

"Funny," Bolan said, "but that's exactly the kind of thinking Fahzal uses."

The BR man lunged with his knife. Bolan sidestepped,

slashing the incoming arm and walking his blade across the man's chest. He slashed up and across the neck, then back again. The thug went down, bleeding out and reeling in sudden traumatic shock.

Bolan kept moving laterally and forward, putting the second man between himself and the remaining three beyond the adversary. He shoved the knife out and through the neck of the nearest man before the BR killer could do much more than gesture with his blade. Yanking the knife free, Bolan pulled the dying man past him and used the momentum to bodycheck the next foe.

He hooked this next enemy's head with his knife arm and flexed, controlling the man's head and driving him downward into a vicious thrusting knee to the gut. The BR killer expelled air and collapsed.

Surging up from one knee, the Executioner rammed the blade up under the jawline of the fourth man. He let the knife go as the man fell.

When he came up again the Desert Eagle was in his fist.

The fifth man froze.

"Drop it," Bolan said. He thumbed back the hammer of the Desert Eagle for emphasis.

There was murmuring among the hash and opium fumes, in the darkness of the cantina. Suddenly, Rosli and his revolver were there. He stood back-to-back with Bolan and leveled his gun at the crowd.

"There will be no calling for help," Rosli announced. "There will be no further violence. You will go about your business and we will leave. We will not return."

"Where were you?" Bolan said quietly.

"Under the table," Rosli admitted, almost sheepishly. "Is that not how you would have done it?"

Bolan almost smiled at that. Still watching his new prisoner, he knelt and retrieved his knife, wiping it clean on the dead man's clothing.

Leaving the fallen BR men to recover or die as fate determined, the Executioner pushed the last man out through the back of the cantina, to the alley behind. Rosli covered their retreat.

Rosli had parked their vehicle in the alley. Where it had come from, Bolan didn't know. It wasn't stolen, but Rosli hadn't had to go far to get it once Bolan had escaped the school. The soldier could only assume his CIA guide had kept a backup vehicle parked somewhere in the vicinity, just in case. It was the sort of thing a good agent would do, and Rosli was proving himself to be that, certainly.

Rosli got in the driver's seat, while Bolan, covering the prisoner, pushed the man into the back. Once they were underway, with Bolan's Desert Eagle shoved into the BR man's ribs, the Executioner explained to him what they needed.

"You're going to tell me," Bolan said, "where I can find your leaders."

The man replied in Malaysian. He either did not or would not speak English, but he seemed to understand it readily enough.

"He says," Rosli said from the driver's seat, "that he will tell you nothing."

"Tell him I know," Bolan said. "Tell him I just enjoy torturing people to death."

"Do you wish me to joke with him, or make him believe it?"

"Make him believe it," Bolan said.

Rosli repeated the threat. The BR man scoffed at that. Bolan shrugged. He reached out, grabbed the man's hair and yanked his head back, shoving the triangular muzzle of the Desert Eagle into the man's open mouth.

"Tell him you've seen me do this before," Bolan said calmly. "Tell him I'm going to kill him unless he agrees to listen."

Rosli relayed the message. Bolan removed the pistol and the BR man began to say something very quickly.

"He indicates he will be only too happy to listen to you," Rosli said.

"Tell him I'm tired of him pretending not to speak English, too," Bolan said flatly.

"I will listen! I will listen!" the BR terrorist started shouting.

"Good," Bolan said. "Now, do that, and do it very carefully." He waited while his prisoner began nodding furiously. "I am working to stop Fahzal's government from massacring countless innocent Indian and Chinese Malays. You know that Fahzal has threatened to burn down the ghetto between Petaling Jaya and Kuala Lumpur. He'll kill everyone in it, and he's using your group's kidnapping of his son to garner support for this genocide."

"You…wish to stop it?" the BR man said, confused.

"That's right," Bolan said. "I have no use for thugs of your kind," he said frankly. "But you are not my goal. I want to keep the peace in Malaysia, and to do that, I need to get Fahzal's son back. You're going to tell me where to find your leaders. I need to talk to them, and I need to do it fast."

"I cannot trust you."

"You can," Bolan said. "You can trust me to put a bullet through your head once I'm done cutting pieces off of you. But you can bet I won't do it quickly. By the end, you'll be begging me to kill you. You'd be amazed how long someone can last, if you're careful about blood loss as you take pieces of them forever."

This was all a bluff. Bolan would no more torture a prisoner than he would kill an innocent. Thugs like this BR terrorist, however, had one thing in common: they thought everyone valued human life as little as they did. Such a man, especially after seeing Bolan knife his way through several of his BR comrades, would have no problem believing Bolan could do something so vicious. The Executioner was counting on that.

"You must agree not to harm any of my brothers," the BR man said.

Bolan gestured with the Desert Eagle. "No deals. No bargains. Tell me where to find your leaders, or the fun starts." He snapped open his knife for emphasis.

"I would do as he says, my friend," Rosli said sadly. "I have watched him murder far too many people over the years. It is nothing to him. He would as soon take your fingers and your eyes as he would look at you."

Bolan said silent thanks for Rosli's acting ability. If he had to guess, he'd say that it was this that put their prisoner over the edge. He started speaking quickly in Malaysian.

"You getting all of this?" Bolan asked the CIA operative.

"Yes," Rosli said. "We can be there very soon."

"Good," Bolan said. He put the knife away. "Find us a nice quiet place to pull over, first. I want to put this one in the trunk."

The expression on the BR man's face was enough to start Rosli laughing.

7

"Our sources verify your local intel, Striker," Barbara Price said over the Executioner's secure satellite phone. Rosli drove as Bolan conferred with the Farm, comparing notes. He had already related the details of the operation so far.

"Can you confirm the location?"

"Only that BR's leadership has repeatedly been rumored to have several assets in Petaling Jaya," Price said. "That is like saying rain is rumored to fall from the sky. It's not exactly a surprise to anyone."

"Understood," Bolan said. "What can you tell me about the leaders themselves?"

"We don't have much we didn't already transmit," Price admitted. "I'm sorry, Striker. This is starting to sound really…"

"Half-assed?" Bolan said, humor in his voice. "Don't worry, Barb. I knew what I was getting into. I knew there were certain exigencies, as Hal might call them. Fortunately our liaison here is turning out to be very helpful. He says the BR has two leaders, which matches what Hal sent before."

"One is Chinese, the other Indian," Price confirmed.

"Cheung is a Chinese Malaysian about whom we know very little, not even a full name. There's also Rajiv Singh, born to a wealthy Indian Malaysian family. He got mixed up in a series of increasingly radical freedom-fighting organizations through the years, culminating in cofounding the BR with Cheung. By all accounts he's a complete sociopath. Don't let their causes fool you, Striker. The BR is like a lint trap for the most vicious, miserable killers Southeast Asia has to offer."

"Don't worry, Barb," Bolan said. "I've seen it first-hand. Has there been any more word from Fahzal's government? Anything about the deadline?"

"Not so far," Price said. "We figure Fahzal's keeping his options open. It may even be an empty threat, just something he gambled with to try and get his son back."

"Maybe," Bolan said. "But I don't like it. Something just doesn't fit, Barb, and I'm damned if I can figure out what it is. Keep me informed."

"We will. We're redirecting that care package to you, now that the courier has had time to get in-country."

"You have the location in Petaling Jaya," Bolan said. "He can meet us nearby?"

"He'll be there, yes," Price said. "And Striker?"

"Yeah."

"Be careful."

"I'll do my best," Bolan said. "Striker out."

He closed the phone. Rosli pointed out the wind-shield. "We are nearing the location our reluctant in-former gave us," he said. "If the safe house truly holds any members of the BR leadership, it will likely be Cheung. The other founder, Singh, has been rumored to be out of the country on some sort of business. No one knows what. At least, no one who will tell *me*."

"I just need to find somebody who can tell me where Jawan is," Bolan said. "I don't intend to leave that boy to die. His father may be a genocidal bastard, but no child deserves to be a pawn in somebody's political game. He doesn't deserve to die."

Rosli nodded.

They sat in silence for a time as they traveled. Eventually, Rosli spoke up. "We have picked up another tail, Mr. Cooper," he said.

"That will be one of mine," Bolan said. "Find us a reasonably quiet spot and pull over."

Rosli nodded and did as Bolan asked. No sooner had they stopped than the car following them pulled up next to them, so close that neither Rosli nor the tail would be able to open the doors on the sides facing each other. The passenger window of the tail vehicle rolled down, and the man inside—he was leaning across from the driver's side—motioned for Rosli to roll down his own window. The CIA operative did so, and the other man started feeding him a very large, very heavy duffel bag.

"I'll take that," Bolan said. The bemused Rosli slid the bag over to him. As soon as the duffel cleared the tailing car's window, the driver stepped on the gas and took off.

Rosli blinked. "Such manners."

"He's a courier," Bolan told him. "They aren't paid to loiter. They tend to stay alive a lot longer if they keep moving."

"How well I know the feeling," Rosli laughed. "What have you there?"

"No offense," Bolan said, removing his weapons, "but I'm going to trade up."

"I know how a man of your caliber prefers to have

his own equipment," Rosli said. Bolan looked at him, wondering if Rosli realized he had made so subtle a joke. The soldier decided it was unintentional.

The duffel bag contained a short-barreled M-4 carbine with an adapted 40-mm grenade launcher. A large supply of loaded magazines, clamped together in pairs, was also included, as was a bandolier of grenades for the launcher. John "Cowboy" Kissinger, the Farm's armorer, had included a handwritten note. It said simply, Don't get shot.

"Impressive," Rosli said, looking at the rifle.

Bolan tucked it back in the duffel bag, which was the only thing he had to conceal it. He put the bag on the floor between his legs.

"We will be there shortly. I suspect I should wait by the car and prepare to flee on your return?" Rosli asked.

"Probably a good idea," Bolan said. "It's going to get hairy."

"This, I have not heard before," Rosli said. "But I understand."

The CIA operative finally brought the car to a halt, pulling into the shelter of a small ground-level parking area. "It is one block, that way—" he pointed "—north."

"Keep your eyes open," Bolan said. "I don't want to come back and find you with your throat cut."

"I would never be so rude," Rosli said.

Duffel bag in hand, Bolan made his way toward the safe house. Their "informer," as Rosli had called him, had given them a fairly detailed description to go with the address. Bolan was confident he would recognize the structure when he saw it.

There was some foot traffic in this mixed commercial

and residential area, but nothing too extensive. The Executioner was grateful for that. He did not want to risk innocents being caught in the cross fire. As it was, he was going to have to get intense quickly. There was still the time limit to consider, and he did not have the luxury of being subtle. That meant that, again, he was going to have to dodge the Royal Malaysian Police, for they would likely be called at the first sign of serious trouble.

And there would be serious trouble.

He approached the house and circled around to the back. There was no activity outside, but he did not expect any. If the BR leadership was holed up inside, they would not want to draw attention to that fact.

Bolan took out his phone and double-checked the pictures of Cheung and Singh, memorizing the facial features of each man. He replaced the phone, unlimbered the M-4 and hopped over a small fence that protected the backyard of the building.

He was committed. It was time to take the battle straight to the terrorists.

It was possible that an armed homeowner, even in a nation where the citizens did not necessarily enjoy a constitutional right to keep and bear arms, might see a man carrying an assault rifle through his backyard and fire a shot at him. But when several automatic weapons opened up from the back window of the target house, Bolan knew he'd found the BR.

The sound of the window being broken out tipped him to the coming explosion. He hit the grass as bullets tore the air above him. There were at least three guns, two of them submachine guns, one of them something heavier. The sound was the unmistakable metallic clatter of a full-auto Kalashnikov, something he'd heard countless times from either end of the weapon.

He could only assume they had been keeping regular watch of the exterior. They might even have closed-circuit television rigged up. He hadn't seen any cameras, but that didn't mean anything. Those could be hidden easily enough.

Lying prone in the grass, with bullets ripping up the soil around him, Bolan angled the M-4 and triggered the grenade launcher.

The 40-mm high-explosive grenade punched a hole in the wall of the house that raised a choking, blinding cloud of black smoke. Bolan lowered his head and let the cloud pass over him. He had seen the effects often enough to know by rote what to expect. The gunfire from inside the house immediately stopped. There was little chance the gunners at the window had survived.

The two-story Colonial-style house quickly became a hellscape as small fires ignited inside. The Executioner put the M-4 to his shoulder and followed it in, half-crouched, ready for anything.

A wounded man with a pistol lurched out from behind the broken wall as Bolan stepped inside. The Executioner put a single 5.56-mm round through the man's forehead.

Two more shooters popped up from hiding, braced behind a kitchen table turned on its side. Bolan fired over their heads and, when they ducked behind the table, he fired on full-automatic through the table surface. The NATO-standard rifle rounds easily punched through the wooden table surface to strike at the men behind it. They never knew what hit them.

He took the stairs leading up to the next floor. There were three with handguns and one with a Kalashnikov on the upper level. Their bullets went wide when Bolan sprayed the M-4 up and over the staircase, driving them back. He took the remaining steps two at a time and then punched each man center-of-mass, letting his assault rifle lead him.

He was standing on a landing that led to an open doorway to his left—nothing and nobody there but the men he had just shot—and a closed doorway to his right. That would be the last remaining place to hide. He was risking taking a round, but again, he did not have time to play it safe. He took a step back and planted a kick solidly next to the doorknob.

The shock of hitting the reinforced door traveled up his leg.

Bolan paused and examined the barrier in front of him. What had appeared to be a simple, wooden door was in fact a reinforced steel door with a wooden veneer. This safe room could easily house the BR leaders…or it could be completely empty. Bolan paused and tried to listen, but he couldn't hear anything, and his eardrums were too bruised from the grenades and automatic gunfire to allow for much beyond a dull roar.

The quarters were too close; he couldn't use a grenade or he'd blow himself up and probably kill whomever was on the other side of the door. There was no handle on this side, now that he looked closely. The doorknob that was part of the safe room's camouflage was made of wood painted to look like brass. It fell free when he reached out to touch it. It was connected to nothing but the wooden veneer.

Bolan knew that the open warfare in this neighborhood would bring authorities, and quickly. He had to take action.

He examined the seam in the door. Removing his

knife from his pocket, he opened it and inserted the blade into the seam—

The knife blade stopped short.

Surprised, he tried several different points in the seam. It quickly became apparent that the steel door wasn't a door at all, but a simple metal plate. It meant the entire thing was a decoy.

Bolan ran for the stairs and leaped from the top to the ground floor. He looked left, then right. Somewhere there had to be a hidden access of some kind. If the metal decoy door was meant to keep searchers occupied on the top floor, the basement was the logical location for a real escape route.

He checked the living room, then the kitchen. There was nothing to see. Then he saw the refrigerator. It was the only thing large enough to hide a doorway, unless there was a trapdoor somewhere in the floor. The floors were hardwood and seamless; that didn't seem likely.

He grabbed the unit and pulled with all his might. The appliance moved much more smoothly than it should have, almost flying in a tight arc. It was set on a rolling track. Bolan found a hatch behind it. He reached out and grabbed the door handle.

The electric shock that traveled through his body was enough to stagger him. He reeled, hanging on to his M-4 with one fist, the numbness in his arm slowly becoming a spreading, prickling pain. Shaking it off, he backed up and emptied the magazine of the M-4, aiming for where the handle lined up with the seam around the hatch.

When he thought chances were good he had broken whatever wire was connected to the door, he again tried his front kick. This time, the hatch gave easily, almost breaking free of its damaged hinges. Inside, small lightbulbs illuminated a very steep, narrow staircase leading down.

An escape tunnel.

Bolan charged down the tunnel, taking the steps in long, distance-eating strides.

He almost missed the trap at the base.

At the last moment, he spotted the serrated teeth of the spring-loaded device that resembled nothing so much as a scrap-metal bear trap. He managed to jump over it and land on the far side. The vibrations as he hit the floor of the dirt-floored tunnel were enough to set off the trap. It slammed shut with a metallic clatter that reverberated through the small space.

Removing his tactical light from his pocket, he illuminated the tunnel with its bright, white beam.

The tunnel extended for several yards and then made a sharp turn. He had to hunch to stand in it, but it was actually fairly large for such a makeshift escape route. Small, battery-powered lights dispelled just enough of the darkness to allow for the BR terrorists to avoid their trap and navigate the tunnel.

Bolan slung the M-4 over his shoulder. The quarters were too cramped for the rifle to be the best choice, and the grenade launcher would be suicide. He drew the Beretta 93-R and, with the light in his left hand, advanced down the tunnel with both light and weapon extended before him.

He swept the tunnel floor, walls and ceiling as he went. There could be booby traps anywhere; he was not going to blunder across a trip wire or step on a buried mine if he could help it.

He risked a glance around the corner of the L-turn.

A shotgun blast echoed through the hallway. It tore into the dirt of the corner, splintering the wood of the brace that held it back. Bolan flinched back with his eyes closed, avoiding the worst of it, preventing any serious damage. He blinked the grit out of his eyes.

Someone shouted down the hallway in Malaysian.

"Come on out," Bolan said. "There's nowhere to go and I'm not going to stop."

"Who are you?" came the answering yell, in heavily accented English.

"I'm trying to stop Fahzal from wiping out the Indian-Chinese ghetto," Bolan said. "But I need to find his son to do it."

There was no reply.

"Help me stop the killing," Bolan said. "If Fahzal doesn't get his boy back, he's going to burn the ghetto down. There's no telling how many might die. The BR attack on the school in Kuala Lumpur has public sympathy riding with Fahzal. If he can tell the world his boy has been taken, even killed, there'll be plenty who support his decision when he cracks down. He could massacre thousands and it might get swept under the rug. Do the right thing."

"The boy is ours!" The shout was punctuated by another shotgun blast, this one fired blindly.

The sound of a hatch opening and closing echoed down the tunnel.

Bolan hurried around the corner. It was empty and terminated in a ladder leading up. If Bolan judged the angle correctly, it would lead to somewhere in the front yard of the target house. He scrambled up the ladder and pushed against the trapdoor above with his shoulder, scrambling after his quarry.

He heard the sound of a pump shotgun being racked.

8

The blast nearly took his head off. Bolan let himself drop back down the ladder, landing heavily on the tunnel floor below. He gave it a three count and then went right back at it, hauling himself up and slamming the hatch open once more.

He saw the BR man make for the rear of the target house. Bolan pursued, shoving the light into his pocket, trying to draw a bead on the running man but losing the disabling shot as the fleeing figure made the corner of the house.

Behind the target house, the yards of the surrounding houses all interconnected, separated by low fences. Bolan leaped the first fence and poured on the speed. He could have shot the BR man dead several times over, but that would have been self-defeating; he needed the terrorist alive.

As he ran, he realized he was hearing police sirens.

It had been inevitable. Bolan had opened a war in suburban Petaling Jaya; no doubt numerous citizens had flooded the local police with calls.

They kept vaulting fences and running through yards. The Executioner almost tripped over the shotgun, after jumping a particularly high fence. The runner had obviously left it behind. That didn't mean Bolan's quarry might not have another gun of some kind, but it was a promising development—and the soldier was tired of dodging buckshot.

It wasn't hard to follow the twists and turns through the backyard route the runner was taking. There was really only one logical way to go, as dense as the neighborhood was. Here and there Bolan would see an overturned piece of lawn furniture or a bent piece of fencing, verifying he was following the right route.

Then they hit the dead end.

The runner stopped short where three houses butted together, cutting off his escape. The butt of a pistol was visible in his waistband, behind his hip.

"It's over," Bolan told him, approaching. He kept the Beretta trained on his quarry, but he dared not deal a killing blow; he needed the information this man might have. "Turn around. Slowly."

The police sirens were growing louder. In the distance, both men could hear voices shouting to one another. That would be the police, coordinating a search, probably fanning out from the target house and the destruction wrought there.

The man turned.

"Cheung," Bolan said. "Give up the boy. Do it now."

"I cannot do that." Cheung shook his head slowly. He started to reach behind his back.

"Don't," Bolan warned. "Don't make me."

"You do not understand," Cheung said. "You will never understand. You of the West. You and your CIA and your global domination. You are so willing to interfere when it suits you, yet we suffer here under Fahzal and you do nothing. We must fight him. If taking his son means we must kill him to show the world, then we will do so."

"But killing Jawan doesn't help your cause," Bolan told him. "You fools are creating *support* for Fahzal! You can't hold children hostage, strap bombs to their teachers and threaten to execute them in cold blood and expect to gain popular support."

"Our methods are bloody," Cheung said as he nodded slowly. "But the enemy we fight…that enemy is bloodier." He went for his gun.

The Executioner could see, in his mind, the shot he would have to make. Already, the marksman in him was computing speed and angles, bringing the Beretta up for a shot that would punch through Cheung's shoulder and render his gun arm useless. If he could just line it up in time—

The bullet hole that appeared in the center of Cheung's chest brought an expression of wide-eyed shock to the BR leader's face. He crumpled to his knees, then fell on his back, with his legs folded awkwardly beneath his body.

Bolan had never pressed the Beretta's trigger.

The police appeared, surrounding them both, pointing guns at Bolan, demanding that he not move, that he lie on the ground, that he relinquish his weapons. The Executioner had waited too long. So intent was he on his only viable lead to the boy, that he had failed to escape when he should have. Now he was surrounded.

The Executioner operated according to a very strict moral code. Among other things, he had vowed long ago never to take the life of a police officer who was just doing his job. There were plenty of times when Bolan's activities had put him on the wrong side of law enforcement. There had been times when entire task forces had been devoted solely to the goal of stopping him, of bringing him in to face justice. Though there had been plenty of times when a few bullets stood between Bolan and freedom, he would never kill a cop for trying to bring him in.

That did not mean, however, that he would not fight back.

He still had a job to do. He couldn't afford to let the local police hinder him. Jawan's life and, by extension, the lives of everyone in the Chinese-Indian Malaysian ghetto, depended on Bolan's freedom to act on their behalves.

The cops moved in on all sides. Bolan waited for them to do so and then lashed out.

He slammed an elbow into the side of the closest man's head, while simultaneously throwing a kick into the stomach of a second. Rolling through the crowd of them, he punched, he threw edge-of-hand blows, he threw palm heels. He stomped and kicked and he smashed with his elbows, again and again. He took each cop down in turn, counting on the melee and the crush of bodies to work in his favor, hoping none of them would try to take a shot at him. The police were earnest and there were at least a half dozen of them, but Bolan was much more motivated and experienced. It did not take long before all of the police were lying in the grass, dazed and moaning or completely out cold.

He had been careful not to hurt them too badly. Some of them would have injuries, yes, but nothing that would not heal. Unfortunately the same could not be said for Cheung.

He went to where the BR leader lay unmoving. When Bolan checked his pulse, Cheung's eyelids fluttered.

Finally, he opened his eyes and was able to fix his gaze on the soldier.

He was dying. He did not have much time. Bolan had seen so many people close to death he knew when the Grim Reaper was knocking. Even if medical attention had been available immediately, there was no saving this man

"Cheung," he said. "Cheung! Listen to me. I can stop the killings. I can stop them from slaughtering your people. But you've got to tell me where Jawan is. Don't let the information die with you. We can put an end to this here, if you just tell me."

Cheung looked at him, hard, and for a moment almost looked as if the anger welling up within him was giving him renewed energy. It faded as quickly as it had appeared. The death rattle was almost escaping him when, with his last breath, he said, "Singapore. Jawan is in Singapore. The Blue…Moon…"

Cheung stared glassily in death.

Bolan said a silent thank-you to the man who, vile terrorist though he may have been, had chosen to do the right thing in the end.

Either that, or he thought whoever was waiting in Singapore might succeed in killing Bolan, in which case Cheung would have some measure of revenge from beyond the grave.

It hardly mattered. If Jawan truly was in Singapore then Bolan would get to him, trap or not.

The Executioner backtracked the way he'd come, careful to avoid showing his face on the street. Eventually he worked his way back to Rosli. He put his M-4 in the backseat of the car and the CIA operative drove away, headed out of Petaling Jaya. He was careful not to drive too fast or to draw attention to himself.

"Did you learn anything, Mr. Cooper?"

"Singapore," Bolan told him as they drove. "'The Blue Moon.' That mean anything to you?"

"The Blue Moon is a very elaborate restaurant in the downtown core of Singapore City," Rosli told him. "I have never heard that the BR are in any way connected to it. I suppose that would make it a very effective place to hold Jawan, if such were the case."

"I'll get my people on it," Bolan said. He dialed the Farm, waited for the scrambled connection to go through and then said to Barbara Price, without preamble, "Rajiv Singh and something called the Blue Moon in Singapore. Can you tell me if there's a connection?"

"We'll get right on it, Striker," Price said. "I'll call you back."

"Do it." Bolan hung up.

"If it is Singapore to which we must go," Rosli said, "I will make arrangements. Dire as things are, we will both need to rest for a few hours this night. I can find us a place and we can take Singapore fresh, in the very early morning."

"No CIA safe houses," Bolan said. "You said yourself that your network is shot full of holes."

"I will find us a hotel and check us in under a clean alias," Rosli promised.

Bolan consulted his mental memory banks concerning what he knew of Singapore. The downtown core of Singapore City was extremely urban and extremely dense, full of skyscrapers. It was a bustling economic and commercial center.

Somewhere in the midst of all that was Jawan, still being held by the BR. Bolan would be glad to smash the organization utterly. He had no use for "freedom fighters" who killed innocents.

"Cooper," Rosli said, "we have picked up a police tail."

"Do they know we're us?" Bolan asked.

"I believe so," Rosli said. As he spoke, the sound of the pursuit car's horn began bleating behind them.

"We've got to lose them. Can we do it?"

"I am an excellent driver, Mr. Cooper," Rosli said with a smile and a wink. He put the accelerator of the compact car to the floor and they shot forward.

Rosli guided them away from the worst of the traffic, whipping the small vehicle around tight corners and into narrow alleyways. A couple of times Bolan thought he would clip the side mirrors of the car, but Rosli's estimation of the vehicle's width was more accurate than the soldier's. They managed to stay ahead of the police cars for a little while, but at each set of crossroads they encountered, more appeared.

"They have us pinpointed," Rosli said. "They are sending more cars to intercept us. We will not be able to keep this up for long."

"Then we're going to have to do something about it," Bolan said. He grabbed the M-4 from the backseat, shouldering the bandolier of 40-mm grenades.

"You mean to destroy them?" Rosli asked.

"No," Bolan said. "I mean to put some things in their way."

Rosli kept the car as steady as he could. The police began shooting from their cars; bullets ricocheted off the roof and one punched through the passenger-side mirror. Bolan aimed carefully with the grenade launcher.

He had to wait to get the shot he wanted, but as Rosli floored it and they pulled ahead, he caught the break he needed. There was an old Peugeot parked at the mouth of a very narrow alley, looking all but abandoned. Bolan aimed, held his breath and punched a grenade into the car, at an angle. The explosion ripped a deep hole in the paving and knocked the body of the Peugeot into the alley.

"Excellent work, Cooper!" Rosli called, watching in the rearview mirror.

"Keep going!" Bolan yelled.

They continued to navigate through the narrow, complex street patterns. Several times Rosli had to stop abruptly and burn rubber to back out of a dead end. Bolan used this to their advantage. Not just once, but twice, he managed to use parked cars to block the police into one of the dead ends, while ducking bullets as Rosli backed his way around the cop cars at full speed.

The little compact was beginning to look like something out of a shoot-'em-up movie. Bolan was already bleeding from the few minor scrapes he'd taken during the assault on the school. He managed to accumulate a few more grazes as he rode half in and half out of the passenger-side window, using his grenade launcher to make things difficult for the pursuers.

"I think they must think you a terrible shot by now," Rosli said, grinning.

"I'm glad you're having a good time," Bolan replied.

Between the CIA operative's driving and Bolan's use of the grenade launcher, they managed to leave all of the police cars behind. In the distance, Bolan could see plumes of smoke, the results of their high-explosive counterpursuit techniques.

They found a small underground parking garage with no attendant on duty. Rosli drove them to the lowest level. Using the duffel bag to carry the M-4 once more, Bolan gladly left the car behind. It was far too conspicuous in its heavily combat-damaged state.

Rosli produced a multitool and quickly traded license plates on two cars. He repeated his hot-wiring routine on the more nondescript of the two compact hatchbacks. The car's alarm started to go off when Rosli got the engine going, but he reached under the dash and pulled something free that silenced the security system.

"We go," Rosli said. "I know a nice hotel, very inexpensive, reasonably clean."

"We don't have a lot of time to waste," Bolan cautioned.

"I know." Rosli nodded. "But not even you can fight forever. And from the look of you, we shall need to use my first-aid kit to patch you up. You are leaking all over the upholstery."

Bolan looked down and realized that he was bleeding from several superficial wounds, and noticeably so.

"Don't worry, Mr. Cooper," Rosli said. "I am an excellent nurse."

"If your first aid is anything like your driving, I think I'll do the bandaging myself."

"How is it that they say it?" Rosli chuckled. "'Everybody is a critic.'"

9

Night had taken the Indian-Chinese ghetto, which brought a certain amount of comfort to Prime Minister Fahzal. He did not like to be seen near the place. The smell alone was enough to make him feel ill. He did not understand how such people managed to live like that. He supposed Nasir was right; they were just naturally mentally and physically inferior.

He counted himself lucky to have Nasir to run his security forces, to see to the day-to-day operations of unpleasant tasks like this one. It left Fahzal free to run the business of the Malaysian state, as it should be. A prime minister should be above such mundane and even vulgar concerns. Nasir never took issue with anything Fahzal required of him; it was yet another reason he was invaluable. And the man was loyal to a fault, always solicitous of Fahzal's requirements, always eager to take on more work, more burdens, if only it would make Fahzal's life easier. Truly, he was a fortunate man, to have such dependable staff highly placed in his organization. He had always liked Nasir, since the earliest days, when he had pondered his place in politics and Nasir had encouraged him to apply his natural leadership abilities.

Now, he stood poised to usher in a new golden age for Malaysia. His nation would become the shining jewel of Southeast Asia, economically prosperous, diplomatically influential. It was simply necessary, for those plans to reach fruition, that certain blights on their social and economic landscapes be eliminated. Much as it pained him to admit it, there were certain races that, as Nasir had explained to him so patiently, simply weren't up to the task of running their own lives properly. They could not be expected to be anything but a burden to the nation that hosted them, and so they would have to be removed.

At first, when Nasir had explained to Fahzal the Nationalist Party's official positions on these matters, and when he had suggested to Fahzal the best ways to accomplish these stated goals, he had been resistant. It seemed unnecessarily harsh, to manipulate them first into ghettos and then into graves. But Nasir had wisely pointed out that this was only a matter of location, not of action. The Indians and the Chinese would, sooner or later, cause all manner of problems that would require they be dealt with harshly. Fahzal could either do what was necessary early on, moving these lesser races to a central location where they could be dealt with efficiently and quickly, or he could permit them to run amok throughout the Malaysian countryside. When put that way, how could he argue? He had allowed Nasir to compose the policies that had formed the great, unnamed ghetto on whose fringes he was now parked.

In all honesty he did not know how Nasir managed to tolerate being so close to so much filth, day in and day out. The man's strength was limitless, and this, too, was why Fahzal depended on him so much.

Nasir had respectfully requested this meeting, so

Fahzal had felt obligated to grant it. Nasir asked so little, and did so much. Unpleasant as it was, it seemed only right to grant his infrequent wishes. Fahzal liked to think this demonstrated to his security chief how valued he was.

The old church on the outskirts of the ghetto was deserted. It had been abandoned by whatever congregation had used it before the shanties and the crime and the disease and the smell of the ghetto had come crawling to its doorstep. Fahzal thought it an odd place for a meeting, but it was a distinctive landmark; he supposed that was why Nasir had selected it. The prime minister found his security chief waiting near some tents erected by the church. The tents were guarded by members of the Padan Muka, who carried Uzi submachine guns.

Nasir waved cordially and came to the window of the limousine. Fahzal hit the button to roll his window down.

"Prime Minister," Nasir said, smiling. "Thank you for meeting with me."

"Of course, of course," Fahzal said. "What is it you require, Nasir?"

"I simply want you to see the operation, and confer with you on our plans of action," Nasir said.

"This could not be done somewhere less unpleasant?"

"We must never shrink from the consequences of our actions, Prime Minister," Nasir said. "As I know you never do, I assumed you would want to survey things here."

"Well," Fahzal said. "Yes, I suppose that's true."

"Excellent, sir,"

As Fahzal stepped gingerly from the limousine, he jumped at the sound of gunfire from above. The cracks of thunder pealed over the ghetto from the bell tower of the church.

"What is that?" Fahzal said, alarmed.

"Do not worry, Prime Minister," Nasir said. "It is my snipers. They are using night vision to keep in check the dangerous rebels within the ghetto. Whenever they spot armed resistance, they strike from above."

"That sounds like a wise policy," Fahzal said quickly.

"I merely do as I imagine you would require and wish," Nasir said humbly. "I am told Majid and the men are bringing in another group of prisoners. Come, we can go to my tent and watch from the shelter there. You may stand in the shadows so that no one recognizes you. I know it is not befitting the dignity of your office to be observed in this place."

"Yes," Fahzal said, relieved. "Yes, that would be best." Once again, Nasir proved that he always placed Fahzal's needs first. It pleased Fahzal greatly to see this.

From inside the open-flapped tent, Fahzal watched while Nasir moved among his men, issuing orders and generally looking efficient and capable. The man known as Majid, the beast of a fellow who acted as Nasir's lieutenant, drove up in one of the military trucks the Padan Muka favored. Accompanied by guards armed with assault rifles, Majid leaped down from the cab and went to the back of the truck, where he opened the gate. Much cursing and prodding ensued.

Majid returned pushing several prisoners before him, all of them Chinese Malaysians. There were quite a few of them, men and women. Fahzal watched as Majid separated the women from the men. The women screamed and resisted, requiring Majid to beat them with his fists. This subdued them quickly.

"Must he be so—"

"Rough?" Nasir supplied. "I'm afraid so, Prime Minister. They are not like us. They respond to little except pain, fear and their baser instincts. It is the way with inferior ethnicities. I am sure you understand."

Fahzal nodded absently.

Majid separated one of the men from the group.

"Watch this now, Prime Minister," Nasir said. "You will find this most fascinating. You see, we are engaged in a program of applying pressure to the ghetto, using our troops, our raids for prisoners and selective release of some of the individuals we interrogate. Already, the shantytown before us is growing more tense. Soon it will explode. And when it does, we will have the justification we need to destroy it utterly, with everyone inside it."

"You are certain this is necessary?" Fahzal asked.

"Of course, Prime Minister," Nasir said. "I take no pleasure in what I am about to do. I simply do what I must for the good of Malaysia. I live to serve you and your requirements in all things, for in serving you I serve our country."

Fahzal nodded, still distracted.

Majid pushed his prisoner to the ground. Standing over the man, he began kicking him repeatedly. It was clear he was toying with the smaller man, trying to goad him. Fahzal could not hear what the big man was saying, but he could imagine it well enough: fight back! Why don't you fight back? I shall kick you again!

Finally, the prisoner had had enough. He pushed himself to his feet and lashed out with a clumsy kick at Majid's knee. The Padan Muka brute laughed and lunged forward, grabbing the man by the chest and squeezing him in a powerful bear hug. Even from this distance, Fahzal could see the man's skin turn red, then purple as Majid crushed him. Majid's humorless laughter, the barking of a hyena, carried to Fahzal's ears even from this vantage.

"Majid may seem like a mad dog at times," Nasir said. "But he is a very useful mad dog. Word of his exploits carries far and wide throughout the ghetto. They fear him. They tremble and they flee on sight of him. I have had him conducting regular raids on the population, and always we send one or two back to spread the tale. Sometimes we even spare the lives of the women, when we are finished with them, so that they may tell of the horrors they have experienced."

"I should think they would not be eager to talk about what your men find it necessary to do to them."

Nasir looked at the prime minister for a moment, then turned back to the scene before them. Majid threw his prisoner to the ground, then fell on top of him.

"Ah, this will be good," Nasir said. "As you know, Majid is quite the wrestler. It may not be obvious in watching him, but he is applying horrible pain to that rebel's joints. The man will scream for mercy. I believe Majid simply likes to keep his hand in—there is no reason to play with the prisoners like this, otherwise."

Again the prime minister turned to look at Nasir, then returned his gaze to the brutality being demonstrated.

Majid succeeded in making the prisoner howl in pain and scream for mercy. Laughing, he pushed himself to his feet, pausing to throw a kick into the ribs of the man on the ground. The steel-capped boots the Padan Muka wore would be terribly painful things to be kicked with, Fahzal decided. He was sure the force his men were using must be deemed necessary, to properly subdue the dangerous rebels.

The big Padan Muka fighter began stomping the prisoner with those heavy boots. The man first tried to move and to roll over the uneven ground, but Majid was faster on his feet than the prisoner was on the ground. Majid crushed the man under his heels, dropping his foot on the prisoner again and again. Eventually the man's screams and cries stopped altogether. He lay on the ground at an odd angle.

"Who will be next?" Majid roared. "Who shall face me?"

"He is always like that, this Majid?" Fahzal asked.

"Yes," Nasir answered. "It is what makes him valuable."

"I see."

Majid signaled for the Padan Muka guards surrounding the other prisoners to assist him. The men protested, and Majid stepped in and punched one in the throat. That prisoner fell to the ground, clutching at his neck, and unless Fahzal was mistaken, he died.

"Crushed trachea," Nasir said. "Majid is fond of doing that."

Nasir had nothing to say to that.

Majid's violence was a signal to the others. The Padan Muka began to move in on the male prisoners, wielding clubs and expandable batons. They started beating the male rebels while the women screamed and wailed. One man curled into a ball, offering no resistance. He was beaten twice as hard as the others, and eventually kicked and stomped.

"Nasir," Fahzal said, tearing himself away from the scene, "there is something we should discuss. My son…"

•

"Jawan will of course eventually be recovered," Nasir said. "We have always known this. And in the meantime, his capture helps create sympathy for our cause. I am sure you can recognize this. This has been part of the plan all along, to capitalize on the emotions generated by the BR's actions."

"Well, yes," Fahzal said. "It's just that when the school was retaken—"

"That did not go according to plan," Nasir said. "And regrettably so. This is because the CIA has chosen to interfere. My men and I are coordinating with the police to neutralize this dangerous American who is operating among us."

"I think I should file a protest with the American government. That they should dare interfere in our affairs angers me greatly."

"No, no," Nasir countered. "This you must not do. That is not how the game is played, Fahzal. We know that they are interfering. They know that we know. Yet we all pretend it is not happening, even as we take action. They will deny everything, and if we catch or kill their operatives, they will deny all knowledge of them. They will claim the actions are those of lone vigilantes, madmen with causes of their own, or expatriates paid by individuals here, essentially mercenaries. And nothing will change."

"Then what do we do?"

"Do not worry," Nasir said. "I have been tracking these CIA spies since we first got word, through our plants in their network, that they were sending an American troubleshooter to penetrate the school. I will see to it that the CIA agents are killed and that will be that. The Americans will not dare protest, or even to bring up what happened, for to do so will be to admit their machinations."

"But they succeeded in liberating the school, and ahead of schedule," Fahzal insisted. "Their interference altered your plan, did it not?"

"Not materially," Nasir said. "And every plan must have a fluid element, a component that allows for flexibility in the face of adversity. This is why you have me, Fahzal. To worry about these things so that you do not have to."

"It is just that I worry about Jawan."

"Do not," Nasir said. "Jawan will be safe enough. Again, allow me to worry about these things. Continue your periodic addresses to the media, condemning the BR terrorists and confusing their actions with those of the rebels here. That will generate the popular support that we need, so that when we cut out the cancer that is this ghetto at our feet, none will be able to convincingly protest our actions. Those who do will look foolish, protecting dangerous child-killers and terrorists. That has been the key to the success of our long-term goals all along, as you know. The benefits of a common foe, a foe whose actions makes opposition to *our* responses seem foolish at best and insane at worst."

"Yes, yes, of course," Fahzal said. "It is just that I worry about Jawan."

Nasir put a hand on Fahzal's shoulder. "Take my word for it, Fahzal. Jawan will be returned when we give the word. He will *not* be returned a moment early—his kidnapping stands to do us much benefit, and we will continue to use it as planned. Otherwise all of our work has been wasted."

"You are right, of course."

"I am always right, my friend. Have we not, together,

ushered in a new age for Malaysia? It has taken much hard work and many difficult decisions, but we have done it together."

"Yes. Yes, of course."

"Now," Nasir said, "you will see that there are certain benefits even to these difficult actions. Majid is bringing us the women. Come, let us go inside the tents here."

"For what purpose?" Fahzal asked as Nasir led him.

"For this purpose, of course," Nasir answered. Majid appeared at the door to the tent. He held two female Chinese Malaysians by their necks. They had been stripped naked and were shivering in fear.

"Choose one," Nasir said. "They are inferior. What will they know or care? The pleasures they provide will help remind you what they are good for. Clearly, they are of little other use."

Fahzal paled. "I really must be going, Nasir," he said hastily. "You continue to do your best for Malaysia. I have faith in you. You work hard for our nation, and I value this. I must go. Good night."

Fahzal felt almost as if he would be ill. He hurried to his limousine, cringing at the sound of more shots from the snipers in the bell tower. Safe inside his car, he helped himself to a long draught of the wine he kept in an ice bucket in the back. The liquid did not calm him as much as he had hoped it would.

The horrors that Nasir unleashed on even these inferior residents of the ghetto…they would always disturb him. He understood that Nasir worked hard and undertook much, and as such his pleasures might be more cruel than an ordinary man's. Fahzal tried to tell himself that Nasir knew what he was doing, and that if he indulged himself with the prisoners, well, that was

only appropriate as long as it was discreet. The idea of
committing a rape himself, however…that made Fahzal
sick inside. He could not imagine forcing himself on a
prisoner. He could not imagine rutting with a stranger
in that way, especially one who was little better than
an animal. What would his wife say? What would his
son say? They could never know that this was even
discussed. They would not understand that men under
Fahzal's control had to do terrible things in order to
safeguard the nation.

Thought of Jawan again made him concerned. He
had allowed his son to be used in Nasir's plans on assur-
ances that the boy's capture would be closely monitored
by the Padan Muka, that they would be in control of
the situation always. But Jawan was never supposed to
leave the relative safety of his school. If the BR could
smuggle him out during the attack, it meant the Padan
Muka's monitoring of him was far from complete or
foolproof. And if that was the case, what guarantee did
Fahzal have that Jawan would truly be returned when
the time came?

He took another long swallow of wine. The driver
was carrying him away from this foul place, and he was
glad of it. He could but trust in Nasir to do as he had
promised, to deliver Jawan to him. Fahzal reminded
himself that, once it was all over, he would be both
greatly relieved and greatly triumphant. All the horror,
all the difficulty, all the terrible decisions made by men
such as he, men in power, would be well worth it. Once
the plan succeeded and Malaysia was so much better
off, once his regime was that much stronger, once he
had cemented his control that much more greatly, then
it would all be worth it. It would feel good. *He* would
feel good.

10

The Blue Moon was just as Rosli had described it. It was a multilevel restaurant with modern furnishings, lots of colored glass and plenty of neon lighting. The place stood out. It was, according to the Farm, very likely crawling with BR triggermen.

Even at this early hour of the morning, it was clear that the restaurant was very busy. The Executioner was not happy about having to leave the M-4 behind, but a man walking into a restaurant carrying a large duffel bag would draw attention. As it was, he and Rosli were dressed a bit too casually for the clientele of the place. There was little to be done about that. All he could do was brazen it out—and be ready to go for his guns at the first sign of trouble.

He was going to blitz his way through the place, roust the BR and see if he could find Jawan or, failing that, find someone who could give him some hint where Jawan might be. He did not kid himself into believing that Cheung's deathbed confession was the beginning and the end of Jawan's whereabouts. This might be where the boy was held, it might be a trap, or it might be misdirection. There was just no way to know, but they could only play the cards they had been dealt thus far.

Barbara Price had called Bolan and outlined the results of the Farm's research. The Blue Moon was owned by a holding company that was in turn owned by individuals linked to Rajiv Singh. It was a tenuous thread, and the fact that Singh himself was not an owner explained why this particular location had not yet been raided by the forces cooperating with the Malaysian police. Bolan intended to get in and out quickly. There was no reason to cause Brognola any more heartburn than he already had, by getting the locals up in arms.

The big Fed had, according to Price, been working the phones nonstop, trying to deflect inquiries from various entities in and around Southeast Asia who were getting wind of the hot war Bolan was waging. The protests and questions had come from everyone but the government of Malaysia itself, which meant that the Malaysians and Prime Minister Fahzal's operatives were deliberately refusing to acknowledge it. Their refusal spoke volumes. It meant they were dirty, that they had something to hide. Bolan wasn't surprised by that, because the whole game had smelled bad from the beginning. It just remained to be seen how dirty Fahzal and his people were, and what exactly they hoped to gain through their involvement with the mess.

He and Rosli moved quietly and quickly through the crowds outside the restaurant. Rosli had refused anything but his usual revolver; when the real action started he would do his best to get out of the way. That was fine with Bolan, who didn't need extra variables in an already difficult situation.

Price had been able to offer one piece of very valuable intelligence, which was the key to the slim, brash plan the two men were now following. There were records indicating that, sometime after the holding company in question acquired the Blue Moon, significant activity and construction had taken place to expand and renovate the basement of the club. Knowing that, Bolan was gambling that if there were BR troops hidden away in the restaurant, perhaps even guarding the boy, they would be on that lower level. He and Rosli were going to search the restaurant for access to the lower level, then penetrate it.

At least, that had been the plan.

Bolan watched things fall apart the second someone recognized Rosli. The man pointed at the CIA operative and shouted in Malaysian.

The next few moments unfolded as if in slow motion. Men located throughout the main level of the trendy restaurant—stationed along the walls, standing by the bar, even sitting at certain tables—produced a variety of weapons. Men and women, presumably innocent civilians, started screaming when the guns appeared. They ran for the exits. The gunners opened up, shouting to each other in a mix of languages. Bolan was too busy dodging gunfire and reaching for his own pistols to be able to do much more than listen to the enemy's cries.

Rosli quickly went to ground and vanished, something he was very good at doing.

In the heat of such chaos, Bolan knew from deadly experience that there was only one way to stay alive. The key was to keep moving, to be an ever-mobile nontarget, and to gain and keep the initiative. The initiative in a gun battle was like some diffuse, magic force; once you had it, you could keep it easily enough, and your success was much more likely. But if you lost it, you would have hell to pay to get it back, and you might die before you got that chance.

Crouching, his guns in his hands, Bolan started triggering rounds. The big .44 Magnum Desert Eagle bucked in his left fist, while the 93-R spat three-round bursts. The air was suddenly a living thing, hot with projectiles and full of smoke and the smell of expended cartridges. The screams were receding as the civilians cleared out, and for that Bolan was glad. In moments, the situation had been reduced to one man against dozens, a lone American counterterrorist amid the hell of countless foes bearing automatic weapons. It was hell. It was danger. It was unadulterated chaos.

It was where the Executioner felt most at home.

In the heat of a gun battle, Bolan moved by long-developed combat instinct as much as conscious thought. He walked, crouched, fired and took cover, popping up from behind each new concealment to fire with deadly effect into the crowd of gun-wielding thugs.

A distant part of his mind thought how ironic it would be if these men weren't the BR at all, and he and Rosli had simply blundered into some organized-crime hangout, in which mistaken identity had prompted a hellstorm that would eventually claim the lives of every man in the building save two.

He doubted that it was a mistake, though.

They had not managed to surprise the BR once; the terrorists had spotted them, attacked them, come at them each and every time, and yet Bolan's superior skill and his ample firepower had been enough to carry the Executioner through.

Today would be no different.

He shot a man through the head. He punched a .44 Magnum round through the chest of another. He put a three-round burst through the neck of a third. He shot a fourth center-of-mass. As his guns ran low, he took cover, changed magazines from his messenger bag and was up again, never stopping, never ceasing, always fighting.

And then it was quiet.

"Rosli!" he shouted.

"I am here!" The CIA operative emerged from under one of the tables. He caught Bolan's expression and shrugged, smiling. "When it works, it works."

"Fair enough," Bolan said. "Come on."

The carpet of the restaurant was soaked with blood. Bodies lay everywhere. Empty brass and fallen weapons littered the floor. There was not a wall, table, countertop or any other furnishing that was not pocked with bullet holes. Somewhere, smoke alarms bleated insistently, their mechanisms triggered by the gun smoke. The gunpowder-and-guts smell made the restaurant a charnel house. Bolan had seen horrors far more extensive, but there was no denying the enormity of the death that surrounded them.

Rosli gazed around in wonder. "Mr. Cooper, you are a very lethal man."

Bolan said nothing. He gestured for Rosli to follow and they exited the restaurant, headed to the back.

The Executioner reasoned that access to the lower level would have to be controlled in some way, of necessity. There was a glass-doored elevator in the back of the room, but it led to upper levels only. There was a small access stairwell, but again, it only went up.

"Rosli," Bolan said. "Check the upper level."

"Yes, of course," Rosli responded. He hurried into the stairwell and was gone for only moments. When he returned, he said, "Nothing. It is a large, empty room. No one hiding there."

That left only the kitchen. Bolan did not bother pointing that out; Rosli was not stupid.

"A pity we could not take some of them alive," Rosli said.

"They didn't exactly give us the opportunity," Bolan pointed out.

"My famous face among the Malaysian terrorist community," Rosli said grimly. "I may be a liability to you, Mr. Cooper."

"If you are, I hadn't noticed," Bolan said. "Come on. We've got to check the kitchen for access to the lower level. It's got to be there."

"You are right," Rosli said. "If there is nothing below, we must ask what these men were guarding so zealously. They sold their lives dearly. I still cannot believe you, alone, took all of these enemies. If you did not keep doing it I would not think it possible."

"Training and experience," Bolan said. "And a healthy dose of will. That's all it takes to prevail in combat."

"You make it sound very easy."

"It's never that."

They entered the kitchen. Bolan had holstered his Desert Eagle but kept the Beretta before him, ready to shoot again if another enemy appeared. Rosli held his revolver almost casually, but Bolan knew he was far more wary than he pretended to be.

The kitchen was fairly standard for a restaurant of the size of the Blue Moon.

"Cooper, we must hurry. Local police will be here any minute," Rosli said.

"I know," Bolan said. "If we're lucky and we find

the lower level, the BR will have left us an alternative exit."

They searched the kitchen quickly, checking the coolers, the ovens and the floors. They found nothing. None of the big appliances were concealing doors, and there were no trapdoor panels in the floor. Bolan was starting to think they had hit a dead end when Rosli snapped his fingers.

"I have it," he said. "We are being too logical. We must think as the BR think. They are very…what is the word…they are for the melodrama. Freedom fighters from movies."

"What's your point?" Bolan asked.

"Turn things. Everything you can find. Knobs. Switches. Turn everything that moves."

Bolan saw nothing to lose. He began switching on the burners on the nearest stove, while Rosli began tweaking and turning dials and controls.

Finally, when he started hitting the light switches, there was a loud metallic *click*.

The sound had come from one of the coolers, which stood open.

"In there," Bolan said. They entered the cooler. A panel on the far wall had opened a few inches. "This is it," the soldier said.

Outside, they could hear police sirens, and loud voices in the outer area of the restaurant.

"The police," Rosli said urgently. He reached out and closed the door of the cooler, then urged Bolan forward. Once they were both inside the hidden passage, he closed the panel. Placing his finger to his lips, he pointed; there was a narrow stairway leading downward.

They took the stairs to the lower level. As they did so, Bolan screwed the sound-suppressor to the threaded barrel of his Beretta. The tunnel and the lower level beyond were only dimly lit, so the soldier unlimbered his tactical light and prepared to use it. He crossed his gun wrist over the wrist of his left hand, bracing the pistol and the flashlight in a modified two-hand hold.

At the bottom of the stairway was another heavy door, this one made of wood. Rosli tried the door handle. It was not locked. Anything and anyone could be waiting behind that door.

The Executioner looked back up the stairway. There was enough space that any noise from below would probably be muffled. He would have to risk it. He would also have to hope there was an alternative exit. There was no way they could go back the way they'd come, with the police crawling all over the Blue Moon at ground level.

Bolan planted a foot on the door and kicked it inward.

There was a single man, dressed in the camouflage uniform of the BR, standing inside the small safe room. He held a pistol in one hand but, when the door crashed open, he had been more intent on the small, tightly wrapped marijuana cigarette between his lips. The joint fell to the floor as he brought his gun up.

Bolan put a single 9-mm round through his face.

The soldier and his CIA guide stood very still for a few moments, wondering if and when the stairway would come alive with police officers intent on capturing them. Nothing happened. Rosli exhaled, permitting himself a sigh of relief.

Bolan looked around. The room was empty except for a chair and a few cardboard boxes. Some of them held bags of marijuana. The amount was not significant.

"Rosli, check that outer room," Bolan said softly. He

poked around with his flashlight among the debris left behind in the safe room. The place had been cleaned out pretty thoroughly. Judging from the outlines in the dust on the floor, the BR hadn't vacated it that long ago.

"There is nothing out there, Mr. Cooper," Rosli reported. "I gather there is nothing in there, either?"

"No," Bolan said. They were no closer to finding Jawan, and until they did, the stalemate over the Indian-Chinese ghetto could not be broken, at least not officially. He had his suspicions about Fahzal's government and what was going on with the BR terrorists and the alleged ghetto rebels. The news reports relayed to him by the Farm were just a little too pat, a little too easy. He'd been saying all along that something stunk, and it still did.

"Keep an eye on that stairway," Bolan said. He bent to check the corpse of the man who'd been left behind.

"Why was that man here alone?" Rosli said.

"I think our reputation precedes us," Bolan said.

"You mean *your* reputation."

"Possibly," Bolan admitted. He found a cell phone in the dead man's pocket and checked its call history. If there had been any numbers in the log, they had been erased. "This one was probably left behind so he could report back to the BR if we managed to take out everybody upstairs."

"You think they thought this place was too well hidden for us to find?"

"Yeah," Bolan said. "We almost didn't, remember."

"True," Rosli agreed.

"I think they were worried we'd work our way through their people like we have been, if we found this place. Obviously they were worried about just that, or they wouldn't have been armed to the teeth."

"You have them very afraid," Rosli said. "And apparently for good reason. How many BR men have you killed, Cooper? They cannot have much of an organization left, at this point."

"Maybe, maybe not." Bolan shrugged. "The thing about terrorists is that there are always more of them."

"Then why fight?"

"For the same reason you step on a cockroach when you see one," Bolan said. "Doesn't mean there aren't more of them somewhere. Doesn't mean there won't always be more of them. But you don't let one just keep running around alive if you can kill it."

"You have a singular way with words, Mr. Cooper."

"Thank you."

Bolan found a hotel key, complete with a key fob on which was written the name, address and room number for the place. Bolan held up the key.

"A clue?"

"I'm a soldier, not a detective," Bolan said. "But right now this is all we've got. If this guy was important enough to trust to report back on what happened here, maybe his hotel room will contain something else, some piece of information we can use. Maybe we'll even find Jawan handcuffed to the radiator or something."

"The what?"

"Forget it," Bolan said. "Let's see if we can figure out how to get out of here and over to this hotel without being arrested or shot."

11

Ultimately, they had been forced to wait for the police to conduct their investigation and then leave. It was a frustrating several hours later when Bolan and Rosli finally reemerged in the kitchen. During those hours, Bolan had not even been able to confer with the Farm. He had been too far underground for even his powerful phone to receive a signal. As soon as they were aboveground again and had confirmed that the police were gone, Bolan checked in with Price and verified that there had been no further developments. He told Stony Man's mission controller that he and Rosli were headed to the hotel. According to Rosli, it was across town.

"Do you really think it's worth the time?" Price asked Bolan.

"It's all we've got," Bolan said. "If we come up dry I'll check in, see if the team can help me come up with another likely move."

"I'll get them on it, see if we can uncover anything else," Price said. "Watch yourself, Striker."

"Striker out."

They took Rosli's car across town to the hotel. Weapons ready, Bolan led them to the door of the room indicated on the dead man's key fob. The two men arranged themselves on either side of the door.

They would not have the luxury of lingering if a firefight broke out. The city police were on high alert thanks to the massacre at the restaurant. They had listened to news reports on the radio on the way over, Rosli translating where necessary. Any further "military-style actions" of the type the media were reporting on would result in a swift, overwhelming law-enforcement response.

The only thing Rosli and Bolan had going for them was that, according to the news, the police thought a team of commandos or mercenaries must be involved. They would never believe that one man, or one man plus his local guide, was capable of wreaking so much havoc.

Bolan, hand on his holstered Beretta, banged on the door.

"Come in, lover!" a woman's voice called out. She had what sounded like an Australian accent.

Bolan and Rosli exchanged glances.

Shrugging, Bolan opened the door and, still standing aside to avoid any sudden gunfire, allowed the door to swing open.

There were three women inside. All wore lingerie, and all were reasonably attractive. One was Asian, one was a Malay and one was Caucasian—presumably the Australian one. She removed all doubt when she spoke again.

"Well, well," she said, smiling. "I had no idea. Do come in, yes."

The Executioner surveyed the room. These were clearly hookers, apparently arranged by the renter of the hotel room. But where was Jawan?

He could hear the shower running in the bathroom. "He in there?" He jerked his chin toward the bathroom, hoping that the occupant of the shower was indeed a "he" and that they would assume Bolan had business there.

The Australian girl nodded. As Bolan got a good look at her, he realized just how young she was, under all the makeup. The thought angered him. He was only too familiar with the personal tragedies that occurred when women were exploited this way, selling themselves or, worse, sold into sexual slavery by those who promised them big money. More often than not, such girls ended up used up, strung out, or dead.

"Yeah, he just got in." She smiled at him, turning on the business charm. "We've got plenty of time to play. All three of us, if you have the cash."

Bolan frowned. "Not today," he said. He reached into his pocket and pulled out a roll of bills in local currency. He peeled off a few of those and gave them to her. "Get dressed, take your friends and go. Don't come back. You don't want to be here."

Something in the Executioner's tone brooked no argument. The girl looked into his eyes and saw something dangerous lurking there. She wouldn't understand it; she would know the danger was not to her, but she would be uncomfortable anyway. Bolan had seen it happen before.

The prostitutes hurriedly dressed and left. Bolan and Rosli settled in to wait for the fellow in the shower. He would be in for a surprise when he emerged, expecting three hookers, getting only a dour Mack Bolan and a nonplussed CIA operative for his trouble.

The water shut off and, a few minutes later, a man in a towel walked out of the bathroom. He started to say something in Malay. Rosli cut him off, and Bolan was there to gesture with the Desert Eagle to make the point.

"Tell him to have a seat on the bed," Bolan said. "And to keep his hands where I can see them."

"I speak English," the man said, sneering. "I know this one. He is the spy, the one we are warned about."

"I'm starting to think my cover is blown," Rosli said.

"Let's not worry about that," Bolan said as the man in the towel took a seat. "You are with the DR?"

"I am. I am called Jelel."

"Well, Jelel," Bolan said, "I have a problem. I want Jawan, Prime Minister Fahzal's son. I know the BR have him somewhere. I want you to tell me where he is."

"Or what? You will torture me?"

"No," Bolan said. "I'll just shoot you."

"I will tell you noth—"

There was a knock at the door. Rosli went to peer through the peephole.

"It is the hookers," he said. "I think—"

Bolan's head snapped up. "Rosli! Get away from the door!"

The door almost exploded inward, driven by the strength of a handheld battering ram. The men in camouflage fatigues who came in after it wore the same mixture of kit and pattern that the BR terrorists from the school had worn. Bolan had just enough time to process that as he and Rosli were swarmed by at least half a dozen men. The soldier saw, beyond them, the prostitutes looking on, and he knew the hookers had sold them out to the BR, probably just for the extra money.

WHEN THE WORLD CAME BACK into focus, Bolan found himself tied to one of the room's chairs. Rosli was similarly bound. The hookers were gone again.

The BR terrorists stood over them. The hotel room felt very crowded.

"Now," Jelel said. "You will tell me what I wish to know, or I will torture you." He smiled. The others backed up slightly, taking positions around the perimeter of the room. They all had knives or handguns and were displaying them as if eager to use them. Bolan realized that most of the weapons they held were his own, taken from him while he was briefly unconscious.

Jelel produced a lighter and lit it. He squatted next to Bolan's chair. "He," he said, jerking his chin toward Rosli, "is not of interest. We know everything that he knows. His laughable CIA think they have some influence in Malaysia. They do not. They are nothing. But you…" He waved the lighter back and forth in front of Bolan's face. "You we do not know. You, who walked into the boy's school and killed so many men. You, who walked into the Blue Moon and killed everyone inside. Who are you?"

"Matthew Cooper," Bolan said. His eyes never left Jelel's face. He did not follow the lighter with his gaze.

"Well, Cooper, I want to know your *real* name. You will tell it to me. And then you will tell me why you are here in Malaysia, killing my brothers," he snarled through gritted teeth. "Why you are interfering in Malaysian business. Then, when you are done telling me everything, perhaps I will kill you quickly, instead of making you beg."

Bolan's hand snapped out like a rattlesnake. Jelel looked in disbelief at the hand Bolan held up, which

should not have been free. He grabbed Jelel by the throat
and threw himself backward in the chair, taking Jelel
with him, dumping the BR man on top of his body.
There was a brief tussle as the rest of the BR terrorists
began shouting at once, waving their guns.

Suddenly the Executioner was on his feet. His hand
was bloody. A slick, red pool formed on the carpet under
Jelel; he would never get up again.

It was more than the terrorists could comprehend;
they had frozen for the barest of instants. It was all the
delay Mack Bolan would need.

The Executioner threw himself at the closest man,
who held his Desert Eagle. He slammed a front kick into
the man's midsection, doubling him over, and snatched
the hand-cannon from his grasp. Shoving the gasping
terrorist toward the others, he brought the gun up in both
hands and fired, and he did not stop until the deafening
thunder of the Desert Eagle seemed to fill the small
room with its fury.

He made sure to shoot the last man in the knee. The
terrorist screamed and collapsed, clutching his leg.

Bolan paused. Nothing moved except the wounded
man. The Executioner reached out, grabbed him by the
collar and dragged him to the chair in which he himself
had been tied. He righted the chair and sat the wounded
man on it. Then he pressed the hot muzzle of the Desert
Eagle against the terrorist's forehead.

"We've got to go," Bolan said. "We've got to go
quickly. I don't have time to play with you. Tell me
where Jawan is or I'll leave you lying there with your
buddies."

"You will not shoot me," the terrorist said.

"No," Bolan said. "You're right. I won't." He held
up his bloody hand. Then he reached out and grabbed

the man's throat. "Maybe you'd like to spend the rest of your short life on the carpet with Jelel there."

Bolan was bluffing. He did not, would not kill if innocent life, or his own, was not endangered. But he needed to know where to find Jawan, and this was the fastest way.

"All right," the terrorist said meekly. "All right. I will tell you." He rattled off an address. "He is there. He is there. Do not kill me."

"You're sure Jawan is there? Alive and well?" He squeezed the terrorist's throat slightly, as if preparing to tear it out.

"Yes!" the terrorist shrieked. "We have not harmed him! He is alive and well! He is there! He is there!"

Bolan looked at Rosli, who was watching with amazement. Bolan clubbed the man across the bridge of the nose with the heavy barrel of the Desert Eagle. The terrorist fell off the chair and onto the carpet, out cold.

Bolan exhaled.

"Uh…Cooper," Rosli said. "Could you untie me?"

"Sure," Bolan said. He retrieved his weapons, his messenger bag of supplies and the Beretta 93-R, checking each and making sure everything was properly rigged and stowed under his shirt. Only then, when he was certain he could fight back effectively if there were any more surprises, did he cut Rosli loose.

"How did you get free?" Rosli asked.

"Let's say I'm flexible," Bolan said. "I've spent a lot of time tied up, being interrogated. It's actually really difficult to secure someone with just rope unless you know precisely what you're doing. There's always some give to the rope, always a way to wriggle free. The more you do it, the easier it gets."

"I see," Rosli said.

He found Rosli's revolver on the floor, checked it and handed it butt-first to the CIA operative. "Come on. We've got to leave again."

"What of him?" Rosli pointed at the unconscious man.

"What about him? We can tie him up before we go if you want to, but I can't see wasting the time."

"Nor can I," Rosli said. He stepped over, aimed his revolver and put a bullet through the man's head. Then he looked at Bolan as if to gauge the man's reaction.

"If you're looking for my approval, you won't get it," Bolan said. "That's not how I do things."

"Will it be a problem?" Rosli asked.

"No," Bolan said. "It's on your conscience. Now we don't have to worry about him tipping anyone off."

"That was my thought," Rosli admitted.

"Yeah, well, it's still not how I do things."

Rosli had nothing to say to that.

The door was almost coming off at the hinges and it was badly splintered. It fell to pieces as they tried to move it out of the way; the terrorists had simply propped it in place. Bolan looked back at the abattoir that was the hotel room.

"There's no hiding that," Bolan said.

"No." Rosli shook his head.

In the small parking lot, they discovered Rosli's car had been vandalized. All four tires were flat and several belts had been cut in the engine compartment.

"You think the BR did this?" Rosli asked.

"Who else?" Bolan said. He looked around, and all the other nearby cars had been similarly damaged. "They did every car in the lot, just to make sure they got yours."

"We could steal one," Rosli offered.

"We'd have to find one somewhere farther out, first," Bolan said. "With the cops on the way toward us at any minute. Not a good idea."

"Then I will call for another car. I am not without resources here."

"Don't forget the duffel bag with the M-4 in it. Can the car get here fast?"

"No," Rosli said. "We will need to leave on foot and rendezvous with the vehicle some distance away. We can take it from the rendezvous to Jawan's location."

"Then let's move."

"We are making quite a habit of escaping before the police can arrive."

"Yeah, I've chatted with the police already this time out," Bolan said. "The conversation didn't go well."

12

They traveled across the downtown core in the car delivered by one of Rosli's local contacts. It was a risky move, as it was likely to alert the BR, the Padan Muka and anyone else who had reason not to like Rosli and the CIA's interference. It didn't matter. They had an address for Jawan and they were headed toward whatever danger existed; if it found them, they would simply reach it that much faster.

The address, Bolan confirmed with Stony Man Farm as they drove, was a video-gaming parlor in downtown Singapore City, in what was a fairly crime- and strife-torn neighborhood by all relative measures. It was, in short, the sort of place where the BR would hole up with a valuable prisoner, trusting that they had the resources and the will to hold that prisoner against an incursion by law enforcement—or the more brutal Padan Muka. In theory, Fahzal's internal security force did not have any authority in Singapore. In reality, Price reported, there were plenty of wire transfers moving from Fahzal and his people to highly placed figures within Singapore's power structure. These were almost certainly bribes, and that meant Fahzal had laid the groundwork from the start of the Nationalist Party's reign.

Yet the BR had felt secure enough in that city-state to create a sanctuary, which spoke volumes about what either country's government did not control. The BR were thugs, killers, murderers—the very worst sort of societal predators. Yet from all reports they were no worse than the Padan Muka, and in some ways probably not as bad.

Price told Bolan that sketchy but increasingly numerous reports of brutality in the Indian-Chinese ghetto were filtering out from Kuala Lumpur and Petaling Jaya. Fahzal and his troops were not content simply to keep the ghetto contained. The Padan Muka were making regular raids into the ghetto, taking prisoners, committing torture, murder, rape. They were making sure word of their activities got around. They were stirring up the people they had trapped, so that when the ghetto finally exploded, it would look like the inevitable and logical climax of the raid by the BR on Fahzal's son's school. That was how Bolan would play it, in Fahzal's place and with Fahzal's apparently racist bloodlust to motivate him. It made sense.

Something still bothered him about the operation. Something was tickling his combat intuition, something he could not quite articulate yet.

It would come to him. He just hoped it would happen before the situation became too dire.

Rosli was very quiet on the drive across town. Bolan suspected he was second-guessing his decision to execute the last BR terrorist at the hotel. He could understand that. It was a powerful thing, taking a man's life when the choice was entirely yours…when the stakes weren't your life or death, but his and his alone. He'd known more than a few men on the wrong side of the law, predators with bloodlust in their hearts, who'd become addicted to that rush, that feeling of power that was determining the life or death of another human being through nothing more than a few pounds of trigger pull.

Rosli was a good man, though, if Bolan was any judge of character at all. It was very unlikely he would gauge a man wrong, at this point in his long war. He wasn't infallible, but he had known many men and women in the course of his battle against evil. One got to know what made the mind work, during all that. Rosli was a just, earnest fighter on the right side of things. He would find his way. And he would learn to live with what he'd done, because there was no other choice. Bolan was not going to judge him harshly for it, even though he would have made a different choice. The BR terrorists were, after all, killers with much innocent blood on their hands. He would waste no time feeling sorry for them when they got what was coming to them.

It was just the way of things.

"Do you intend," Rosli said, "to simply walk in there and shoot everyone, as you have in the past?"

"It's a thought," Bolan said. "Do you have a better plan?"

"I do," Rosli said.

As it turned out, the CIA's network was a bit more extensive in Singapore than it was in Fahzal's Malaysia, Rosli explained while they drove. If they should indeed find and rescue the boy, Jawan, they would need to transport him back to Malaysia as quickly as possible. He could arrange, with a few well-placed phone calls, for a helicopter and a pilot to be waiting for them at one of the helipads dotting the high-rises of the downtown core. That would improve their escape route—but it was possible that Rosli's CIA contacts could meet them with some equipment that would make reaching Jawan that much easier. He explained what he had in mind.

"Make your calls then," Bolan said. "That's a solid plan."

Rosli smiled. He looked pleased to receive Bolan's approval. He began making calls on his cell phone.

By the time they neared the target, all was ready. A second compact car pulled in alongside Rosli's and the driver tossed a heavy canvas bag in through the driver-side window. Rosli passed the bag over to Bolan, who opened it and checked the contents.

"Looks like it's all here," he confirmed.

"Good," Rosli said. "Then let us be down to business."

They parked the car and made their way, cautiously, to the entrance of the gaming parlor. The streets outside were busy. Bolan was determined to keep the action contained to within the parlor itself. Clearing out any civilians, purging the video-gaming house of BR terrorists and rescuing Jawan—not in order, but simultaneously—was the threefold goal.

Bolan was ready. His weapons were primed. In the canvas bag he had the care package from Rosli's CIA friends. As they threaded their way through the crowd in the entranceway of the video-gaming parlor, Bolan reached into the bag and handed an item to Rosli.

Rosli donned the gas mask, receiving a few odd looks from those in the crowd around him.

Bolan pulled on his own gas mask.

Reaching into the bag, he removed several gas grenades. Some of these he gave to Rosli. The two men walked through the crowd, pulling the pins and tossing the grenades across the floor.

When the grenades started to detonate, a choking cloud of tear gas was produced. The reaction from the curious crowd was instantaneous. People began to cough and wheeze, their eyes streaming. They began fleeing the gaming parlor, headed for the long, low, wide doors of the front entrance. It was the closest thing to an immediate evacuation they were likely to achieve.

Bolan unlimbered his weapons once he had used all of the gas canisters. The gas mask restricted his vision somewhat, but it was far preferable to the unadulterated, unfiltered, unprotected effects of the tear gas. The gas would clear out the civilians flooding the ground floor and, if the intel he had gotten from the Farm was at all accurate, they would be free to tackle the upper level of the parlor. It was that upper level that housed the parlor's administrative offices. There was no basement, no other part of the building. If Jawan was here at all, he would be upstairs.

He had thought the BR troops would be on the defensive, especially fighting through the effects of the tear gas. Perhaps out of desperation, however, they mounted an attack. As Bolan and Rosli approached the spiral staircase to the upper level, several men in camouflage fatigues took those steps two at a time on the way down. They opened fire with handguns and Kalashnikovs, firing blindly through the choking, blinding fumes.

"Down, down, down," Bolan commanded, shouting so Rosli could hear him over the gunfire and distortion of the mask. He gave the CIA operative a shove to get him out of harm's way, then advanced with his Beretta 93-R at the ready.

It was, Bolan would think later, a little too much like shooting ducks in a pond.

The tear gas had the enemy completely disoriented. They blundered about the ground floor, panic-firing into the gaming machines. Two BR gunners accidentally shot each other.

Bolan moved among them like a wraith, placing his suppressed shots with cold precision, drilling each man with a burst through the chest or head. With the protection of his gas mask, it was only too easy.

He ran into Rosli again, finally.

"Are they all dead?" Rosli asked.

"I think so," Bolan said. "Check the floor again. Move along the perimeter and don't get shot in the back. Meet me here."

The fumes were starting to dispel, making it easier to see the bodies of the BR shooters splayed on the floor.

"About now," Rosli said through his mask, "it should be time to remind ourselves that the police are coming, and time is short."

"I think you're getting the hang of this," Bolan said. "Bring the car as close to the front entrance as you can, and keep the engine running. If Jawan is up there I'm going to be bringing him to you, and doing it in a hurry. Even if he's not, we'll need to make a fast getaway, like you said."

"I understand," Rosli said. He hustled off.

Bolan turned to look up the staircase. Holding the Beretta in one hand, he extended his arm and let the weapon lead. Ascending, he kept the top of the stairs at the center of his vision, waiting for the sucker shot that was sure to come.

When it did, he was not disappointed. A BR gunner

popped up like a rabbit, aiming a pistol down the stairway. Bolan put a single bullet through his forehead. The
terrorist disappeared back the way he'd come.

The Executioner found the man sprawled at the top
of the stairs. Directly ahead, a hallway led to the administration offices. The doors of each office were closed.

The trap was obvious.

He would need to clear each door. As he did so, however, he would be vulnerable to attack from behind while
he was focused on each new chamber. If the BR waited
beyond those doors, they would be waiting for him to
make a mistake, waiting to put a knife blade or a bullet
into his back.

There was nothing to do but trip the trap and deal
with the results. Drawing the Desert Eagle with his
left hand, he put his foot against the nearest door and
slammed it open.

The terrorist inside opened fire as soon as the door
slammed open. Bolan was not there, however. As he
shoved the door, he moved to the side, leaving only
his left arm and the Desert Eagle projecting through
the doorway. With the flash sight picture of the gunner's position still firmly in his mind's eye, he put a .44
Magnum slug through the man's neck, almost blowing
his head from his body.

There was no time to turn and no time for anything
fancy. Bolan cocked his elbow and shoved the Beretta
in his right hand upside down, aiming over his shoulder.
He triggered several three-round bursts as he felt the
opposite door being thrown open. The screams from the
BR shooter closing on him told him his aim had been
true.

The second door was a repeat of the first. Bolan
sprayed the room down with bursts from the Beretta,

taking out three Kalashnikov-wielding terrorists huddled within. There was only a single man in the opposite office, and he attacked with a large knife of some kind. Bolan blocked his clumsy overhand thrust with the big metal bulk of the Desert Eagle, pushed the muzzle of the Beretta into the man's stomach and fired a triple blast that blew the man back the way he'd come, toppling the terrorist into the room he had been guarding.

The last set of doors, before the final meeting room, was a bit more complicated. Bolan kicked open one door only to find the room beyond empty. As he was pushing that door open, the one behind him slammed open and several more terrorists streamed out, attacking with knives so as not to risk shooting each other in the crush of bodies.

Bolan fired his guns dry, blasting into their midst, cutting them down as if harvesting wheat. When the weapons were empty and there was no time or space to reload, he let them fall, drawing his knife and snapping it open.

The remaining terrorists were anxious to find his flesh with their blades. He slapped aside the first clumsy slash and speared the knifer in the throat. He slammed the sole of his boot into the knee of another, driving the handle of his knife into the top of the man's skull. He cut the throat of another, sidestepping the spray and driving the stiletto's blade deep into the abdomen of the last. He carved his way out and elbowed this final, unfortunate soul in the back of the skull, not waiting to see him topple.

The final door opened.

Rajiv Singh stood there. Bolan recognized him readily enough from the Farm's intelligence briefing. The BR cofounder had a Makarov pistol in one hand.

He was pressing the muzzle of the gun to a young boy's temple.

"Very good, American," Singh said. He was sweating profusely. Whether nervous, on some substance or simply unhinged, Bolan could not guess.

The Executioner stood there, the knife in his hand the only weapon he had.

"Jawan?" the soldier asked.

The boy nodded solemnly.

"Yes, yes." Singh sounded annoyed. "This is the boy. This is Jawan, on whom so many plans depend, around whom so many great and terrible political intrigues revolve. He is unharmed. He will remain that way provided you stand aside and allow me to leave."

"Can't do that," Bolan said, shaking his head. "Cheung is already dead. The BR is suffering an extreme lack of leadership and a serious depopulation problem. I intend to make that permanent."

The Executioner looked Jawan Fahzal in the eye and nodded.

Jawan nodded back.

"We will rebuild," Singh said calmly. "We will continue to bring the fight to that butcher, Fahzal."

"Butcher?" Bolan asked. "What do you call what your people were willing to do to Jawan's classmates and teachers?"

"Such things are sometimes necessary," Singh said.

"No," Bolan countered. "They never are. And you're not going to do it again. Now, let the boy go."

Singh's expression grew suddenly stern. He extended his arm as if cracking a whip, firing a pair of shots from the Makarov.

Bolan's reaction beat Singh's action. He threw himself into nearest open doorway.

"Jawan!" Bolan yelled. "Go!"

Jawan broke free. As he ran, Bolan stood, leaning out the open doorway.

The Makarov came up in Singh's fist again, tracking the Executioner.

Bolan did the only thing he could do.

He threw his knife end over end.

The big, sharp, needle-shaped blade entered Singh's right eye and buried itself deep in his brain.

He fell on his back, a puppet with its strings cut, staring forever into nothing with his one good eye.

Bolan exhaled.

Jawan approached him tentatively. "Something smells funny," he said, wrinkling his nose. Bolan knew he meant the tear gas. The fumes weren't too bad up here yet, but they would get worse.

"Don't worry, son," Bolan told Jawan. "I have a ride waiting."

13

The Executioner sat with Jawan in the backseat, the boy watching out the window nervously as if he thought he might be picked up again at any moment. Bolan could not blame him. Being taken captive, held for so long, with no control over his own destiny. Even for a young boy, that would be difficult. It was likely Jawan would need some serious counseling to cope with the emotional fallout of his ordeal.

On the positive side, despite the brutality of the BR, and despite their hatred for Jawan's father, Jawan himself did not appear to have been physically maltreated in any way. He had not been beaten, he said he had been given food and water regularly and he had spent his time in captivity playing video games under guard in one of the private administration rooms at the gaming parlor. All in all, it had not been completely horrific.

Jawan, when not watching for unseen pursuers, was looking at the Executioner with a mixture of fear and awe. Bolan regretted that the boy had watched him kill Singh, but there was nothing to be done about that. Much as Bolan would have preferred to spare him the harsh realities, the political climate in which Jawan and his family lived meant that he had been subjected to them, and would be subjected to them.

And it was not over.

"How far out are we from your helipad?" Bolan asked Rosli.

"Perhaps fifteen minutes if the traffic patterns hold."

"I think that's going to be too long."

"You have seen them, too?"

"I think so," Bolan said. He had turned to watch out the rear window with Jawan. The boy pointed.

Bolan nodded. He turned back to Rosli. "We're being followed again. There are three cars, black sedans."

"Do you think the BR followed us?"

"No," Bolan said. "For all intents and purposes, we've broken them. No, I think the Padan Muka have been onto us since you had your people call for this car."

"It seems likely," Rosli said. "They would have been monitoring my activities in order to reacquire us, finish the job they started. Do you think the fact that we have rescued the boy will buy us a reprieve?"

"It might," Bolan said, "but I wouldn't count on it. They'll want to stop us, talk to us and take the boy back to his father, which is fine." He shook his head. "But I think they'll be thinking in terms of tying up loose ends, not expressing their undying gratitude. I think they'll want to bring Fahzal good news and his boy all in one package. 'Here's your son, oh, and we shot those interlopers from the CIA.'"

"You have a way of expressing things very plainly, Mr. Cooper," Rosli said.

"Well, at any rate, they won't start shooting immediately—"

Gunfire turned the rear windshield into a hailstorm

of glass. Bolan grabbed Jawan and threw him to the floor of the backseat, covering him with his body. More bullets punched through the car, one of them shattering the rearview mirror, but Rosli was able to keep control. The car swerved, the tires screaming, and the CIA operative was able to keep them on the road and moving through traffic, swearing softly to himself in Manglish the entire time.

"Mr. Cooper, have I told you that I think you are cursed with bad luck?" Rosli asked, whipping the steering wheel first left, then right.

Bolan drew the Desert Eagle. Bracing his arm against the rear windshield shelf of the compact, he tried to track the pursuing cars.

There was too much traffic. There were too many innocents who could be caught in the cross fire. He didn't dare engage the shooters for fear of taking out innocents.

"Find us a parking garage, some kind of containment structure," Bolan said. "Fast as you can!"

"I saw a sign a block behind us," Rosli said. He brought the car whipping around in a tight U-turn that had the pursuing drivers confused as he broke through their ranks. Bullets raised sparks off the sheet-metal skin of their car, but the tires remained intact.

Jawan huddled on the floor of the car, perfectly silent. Bolan had to admit the boy had courage; he was not screaming or yelling, merely staying out of the line of fire. Watching for his opening, Bolan kept an eye on the cars behind them as Rosli brought them screeching into an underground parking garage whose attendant shouted something at them.

Rosli ignored the attendant and smashed through the wooden tollbooth barrier. He headed down, always down, taking the ramps at dangerous speed. He showed good instincts; it was what Bolan would do, too, and in fact had done in the past.

Eventually, the parking garage dead-ended. "Stay low. Stay with Jawan," Bolan told Rosli. With the Desert Eagle in his hand, he jumped out of the car and started walking toward the ramp leading up and out.

The chase cars came thundering down the ramp. Bolan took shelter behind a cement column as they roared past, then stopped, disgorging several men dressed in civilian clothes and armed with Uzis. They could have been twins to the men he and Rosli had first faced when Bolan had arrived in-country. If these were not the Padan Muka, Bolan would be very surprised to hear it.

How they had acquired Rosli's vehicle, Bolan wasn't sure. They would have to check into that later. But first things first.

The men were shouting to each other in Malay, making preparations to fan out and search the garage. Rosli had parked amidst the other vehicles on that level, but there were not many of them. It was good in that the chances of a civilian blundering into the imminent combat zone were low. It was bad, however, because the shooters would not have many cars to check before they found Rosli and the boy.

The Executioner was going to have to give them something else to think about.

He leaned out from the shelter of his column, drew a bead on the nearest man and fired. The 240-grain slug punched through the back of the man's head and flipped him onto his face on the pavement. The shot echoed through the parking garage.

The return fire was immediate and overwhelming. A

fusillade of 9-mm gunfire chewed up the column behind which Bolan hid. He was soon enveloped in a cloud of dust.

He tried to break cover just long enough to take another shot, but the gunfire was too much; he had to duck back.

He was pinned. There were too many of them.

Just when he was starting to wonder exactly what he was going to do about that fact, a car near the gunners exploded in a spectacular fireball. The shrapnel tore into the ranks of the gunmen and sent several of them sprawling. One man, too close to the car that had detonated, ran screaming through the parking lot, his entire body aflame.

Bolan saw Rosli pop up from behind the line of parked cars. The CIA operative had the M-4 in his grip and was lining up the 40-mm grenade launcher for another shot. Bolan ducked back behind his column when he heard the hollow sound of the launcher discharging.

A second explosion rocked the lowest level of the parking garage. Bolan joined the carnage, drawing his Beretta, firing both guns into the crowd of shooters. He took one man in the face. Another he shot through the chest. Still another he shot through the neck. He fired and fired, scything through them and moving around them, flanking them and making it appear as if they fought many enemies at once. Between Rosli's new love affair with the grenade launcher and Bolan's deadly shooting, the hunters had suddenly, and inexplicably from their point of view, become the hunted.

The shooters had, under the onslaught, lost all pretense of unit cohesion. They began running blindly through the parking garage. Bolan holstered the Desert

Eagle and flicked the selector of the Beretta to single shot. He attached the sound-suppressor to his weapon.

The Executioner began hunting the stragglers through the maze of parked cars and columns. Trusting Rosli and the M-4 to guard Jawan and keep the boy out of harm's way, he instead devoted himself fully to purging the parking level of any gunmen. A few had probably escaped up the ramp, and that was fine; if they weren't there, they couldn't be shooting at Bolan or, more importantly, at Jawan.

Now that they had the boy safe and sound, Bolan did not intend to let anyone take him. The lives of everyone in the ethnic ghetto depended on getting Jawan back to his father in once piece.

That alone would not be enough, though. They would have to find a way to alert the media, to make sure that all of Malaysia knew that Jawan had been returned. With luck that would undercut popular support for the ethnic-cleansing action in which Fahzal's Padan Muka thugs were about to engage. It might even save Jawan's life. Bolan strongly suspected that the Padan Muka were trying to shoot Jawan because he'd been liberated prematurely. It seemed Fahzal himself might be willing to sacrifice his own son in order to achieve his political aims.

The Executioner was a ghost moving among the cars and the dead. The clapping of his machine pistol with the sound-suppressor attached was audible in the garage, but sufficiently muzzled that the shots didn't give away Bolan's position.

Toward the end, the killers were screaming for mercy, losing their minds in fear and firing blindly into every corner of the garage.

Bolan popped up in front of the last of them. He had

been hiding behind a convertible sedan. When he appeared, the shooter shrieked and dropped his gun.

"Don't move," Bolan told him.

The gunner froze.

"Hands up," Bolan said. "Keep them where I can see them." The man complied. "Who do you work for?"

The shooter looked at him as if surprised.

"Cooper!" Rosli shouted. "Are you all right? Do you need assistance?"

Without turning from his new prisoner, Bolan shouted back, "I'm fine. Stay right where you are. I'll come to you." He gestured with the pistol and, more quietly, said to his prisoner, "One last chance. Who are you working for, and why were you trying to kill the boy?"

Again the man looked at him oddly. It was then that Bolan realized the man's ears were bleeding. Apparently he'd been caught too close to one of the explosions when Rosli turned loose the M-4's grenade launcher. The man probably couldn't hear a word Bolan was saying. That explained his confusion.

Bolan gestured for the man to lie down on the pavement. He would frisk the prisoner and then secure him with some of the plastic zip-tie cuffs he carried with him. Then Bolan and Rosli could—

The prisoner suddenly surged upward, slamming into Bolan and knocking him to the pavement. The Executioner lost his grip on the Beretta and felt the weapon being pulled from his hand. Rather than let the gunman use it against him, he fired a kick that sent the gun skittering across the paving. His adversary leaped on top of him and began punching him again and again.

Bolan wasn't about to let someone beat him senseless. Guarding his head with one arm, he reached down, flicked open his combat knife and jammed the six-inch blade of the stiletto into his attacker's side.

The gunman screamed. It was an almost inhuman sound.

Bolan tore the knife free and rolled the would-be killer off of him. The man clutched at his stomach and immediately went pale, sweating in shock.

"It's bad," Bolan told him. "Can you hear me?" There was no response, but he hadn't really expected one. He leaned over the man and made eye contact with him. "I said, your wound is bad. Do you understand me?"

For his attempt to help this fallen adversary, Bolan got more treachery. The man tried to grab him by the throat with one hand while clawing at his eyes with the other.

Bolan, still holding the blade, hammered the man into unconsciousness with the butt of the knife.

He found Rosli standing protectively over Jawan, the M-4 at port arms. "Good work," Bolan said.

"Thank you," Rosli replied. "I asked myself, what would Cooper do, if he were me? And I concluded that you would blow everyone up and then shoot them all for good measure. I see that the plan was, more or less, followed in just that way."

"More or less," Bolan said. "Come on, we've got to leave."

"Once again we remain a step ahead of the authorities."

"Not for long," Bolan said. "I want to get to the chopper, but we're going to be making some calls from the air. We need to make sure of who we're dealing with, then see to it this can't happen again."

"What do you mean?"

"I'll explain in a minute. How do you think they found us before?"

"I assumed either they tailed us, which seems unlikely because neither of us detected it, or they tracked us from afar through some other means."

"My thoughts exactly," Bolan said. Going to Rosli's battered car, he lowered himself to his back and slid under the rear of the vehicle, feeling along the edge of the bumper. He did not have to search long to find it. The transmitter was the size of a pager and boasted a blinking red LED.

"Your car was lowjacked," Bolan said, pulling himself to his feet and handing Rosli the transmitter. "Probably before it even reached us."

"Then conceivably they waited for us to rescue Jawan."

"Before moving on us, yes," Bolan said. "Do you recognize any of them?"

"No," Rosli said. "But look at this." He held up an ID card wallet. "This was in the pockets of one of them." He pointed to a dead man on the pavement nearby. "This man has government credentials. He is identified as a bodyguard to Prime Minister Fahzal. That makes these men Padan Muka."

"Which means this wasn't mistaken identity," Bolan said. "This was a deliberately planned operation. They were trying to endanger the boy, if not shoot him outright."

"But that makes no sense."

"No, it doesn't," Bolan said. "We have to consider the implications for turning Jawan over to his father."

"Surely you do not think the boy's own father means him harm," Rosli said.

"Don't I?" Bolan asked. "Think about it, Rosli. Is

the location and itinerary of the offspring of a head of state usually public knowledge? How did the BR know to attack the school when and how they did? Somebody had to tip them."

"But that is no reason to believe it was Fahzal himself."

"Not by itself," Bolan agreed. "Think about everything this 'kidnapping' has helped Fahzal gain, though. It's gotten him sympathy. It's given him leverage. It's been a very convenient reason for everything he's done so far, up to and including not giving a specific deadline for Jawan's return."

"I do not understand."

"If you were Fahzal," Bolan said, "and your son had been kidnapped, and you issued an ultimatum, what's the first thing you would do?"

"I would demand my son be unharmed."

"After that?"

"I suppose I would tell my enemy that the boy was to be returned by a specific time, after which I would take direct action on the assumption that they would not give him up willingly."

"Exactly," Bolan said. "Yet at every turn he's refused to give a deadline. The only reason to do that is to keep his options open, to see just how long this 'crisis' can be strung along, to see how much political benefit he can accrue."

"It does make a certain sense, Mr. Cooper."

"It does." Bolan nodded. "That's why I'm not about to hand Jawan over to his father and trust his father not to harm him."

"Then what do we do?"

"We involve other entities within the Malaysian government," Bolan said. "Entities he can't or wouldn't have thought to control."

"Such as?"

"What's the equivalent of Child Protective Services here?"

Rosli blinked at him. "Mr. Cooper," he said, a smile slowly brightening his features. "You are a brilliant man."

Bolan had nothing to say to that.

14

The Berjaya Times Square shopping mall was an enormous ten-story building boasting, among other things, Southeast Asia's largest bookstore, several department stores, a large-format movie theater and several other consumer attractions. Bolan chose the public location because, according to the team at the Farm, the upper floors of the mall were still described as "sparse." That translated to "not rented," meaning that after walking the gauntlet of the public mall, anyone with whom Bolan and Rosli met to exchange Jawan could be routed to the upper floors where there were few civilians to get in the way. It was the only way Bolan would agree to do the transfer. He needed a public site, but he needed to make sure no innocent people were caught in the cross fire. The unrented upper floors of the mall were perfect for that purpose.

The helicopter ride back to Kuala Lumpur had been uneventful. Jawan had even enjoyed himself, watching out the window as their CIA-sponsored pilot flew low over the landscape below. The boy was resilient. He would come through this all right, provided they could keep him alive. The Executioner intended to do just that.

"All right," Bolan said, once he and Rosli were camped beyond what would eventually be an information kiosk. Jawan waited with them, looking around in fascination. The concrete-and-wood kiosk behind which they hid made good cover and concealment as they awaited their visitors.

"They'll have to enter through that door at the far end," Bolan said, pointing. "Once they do that we're going to lose potential control over them, especially if they choose to take the opposite stairs there and there—" he pointed again "—and take their chances on the upper level."

"Do you really think it will come to that?" Rosli asked.

"I'm hoping it doesn't and can't," Bolan said. "But that doesn't mean I don't think it's possible."

"I understand," Rosli said.

"The social-services people will be guarded by a contingent of Royal Malaysian Police," Bolan said. "That's the deal my people brokered. They'll protect the social workers and Jawan as they make arrangements to get him to a safe location. There he'll be cared for until this is over and the danger to him has ended."

"Can we trust the police? They could be paid off by Fahzal."

"They could," Bolan agreed. "But if they were so loyal to him that they'd be willing to quietly murder his son for him, he wouldn't need the Padan Muka to act as his backbreakers. I'm willing to bet that bribes only go so far. The police may be bought and paid for, but at the end of the day they're still the police, not Fahzal's private thugs."

"We are gambling with Jawan's life."

"We are gambling with our own, too," Bolan pointed out. "There's always risk. But I won't do anything to endanger Jawan. This is his best chance of getting through this in one piece."

"I agree."

Bolan checked his watch. "It's time. They should be here any minute."

Moments later, the contingent from the government arrived. Uniformed police carrying Kalashnikovs walked in a protective cordon around two Malay women in business suits. The police looked stern, the women nervous. When they were close enough, Bolan called out to them.

"Wait right there," he said loudly. "We have Jawan and we want to turn him over to you provided you can guarantee his safety."

"As was promised," one of the police officers called out. "We shall take the boy and see to his safety until the crisis is past."

"All right," Bolan called back. He turned to Jawan. "Okay, Jawan. Looks like the worst part of this is over—"

The shots that rang out pealed across the largely empty space of the upper floor of the mall, rattling skylight panes in their frames. The bullets tore through the Royal Malaysian Police and the two social workers, throwing their bodies this way and that as they went down in a hail of lead.

"Shit!" Rosli said firmly.

"Agreed," Bolan said, ducking back behind the cover of the kiosk and making sure Jawan stayed down.

There was shouting in Malaysian. From the stairs, several armed men emerged, their assault rifles still spitting lead as the bodies of the dead police and social workers were unnecessarily riddled with still more bullets.

"What are they shouting?" Bolan asked.

"Glory to Fahzal, death to the West," Rosli said sourly. "They identify themselves as Padan Muka. They announce loudly that we shall get what we deserve if we resist, and they demand we turn over the boy."

"I thought it was probably something like that."

"How do you think they found us?"

"Probably followed the group out there," Bolan said. "If I had to guess I'd say Fahzal has spies at every level of his government. When they got word Jawan had been recovered, I wouldn't be surprised if somebody made a phone call straight to the prime minister's residence. I knew that was a possibility but I didn't think they'd go this far. They're as much as saying they want to murder Jawan in his tracks."

The boy looked up at Bolan, eyes wide.

"What do you suggest we do?" Rosli asked.

"Back to plan A," Bolan said.

"Walk over there and shoot everyone?"

"Yeah, that one," Bolan confirmed. "Watch Jawan."

"I shall guard him with my life."

The Executioner made sure both of his pistols were loaded and ready. The M-4 with its grenade launcher was in its duffel bag at his feet. He removed it, listening to the Padan Muka across the floor shouting further threats and demands.

"The instructions have not changed," Rosli reported. "They demand that you surrender."

"Tell them I agree."

"Cooper?"

"Just tell them. Tell them I'm coming out, don't shoot, et cetera. Tell them we're willing to give up the boy in exchange for safe passage out of here."

Rosli shouted as Bolan asked. There was a response. Rosli nodded. "They await you."

"I'll bet they do."

Bolan stood and vaulted the kiosk, his M-4 held in his right hand, his left palm on the surface of the wooden countertop. As he swung up and over, he leveled the short barrel of the M-4 at the crowd of Padan Muka gunmen waiting across the cavernous, glass-walled space.

The M-4 bucked in his fist as he triggered a long, withering blast on full-automatic. Brass rang from the polished floors. Bolan's boots hit that floor and he charged the enemy, running toward them with all the speed he could pour on, his weapon spitting flame and 5.56-mm destruction.

It didn't matter if the Padan Muka gunmen had thought, at any point, that he was seriously considering surrendering. The first rule of warfare was to refuse to make things easy for your enemy—to deny him simplicity, clarity and certainty. The Padan Muka would be struggling to reconcile his promises with his actions, or they wouldn't. The end result would be the same. Mack Bolan charged the guns of the enemy and he began slaying them wholesale.

There was not much cover except for the support columns holding up the roof, which were spaced evenly across the open area. Bolan ran in a chaotic, zigzagging pattern, trying always to keep a column between him and the bulk of the shooters.

The Padan Muka were moving, trying to do exactly the same thing Bolan was doing. They were thugs and they were not exactly professionals, but they weren't entirely stupid. They knew a sound tactic when they saw it, and they mirrored it, trying to take Bolan down.

Bolan, for his part, was not spraying and praying blindly, as the Padan Muka troops were doing. While he used sprays of automatic fire to keep the enemy off balance and drive them back, when he truly wanted to take out a target, he used a compressed, short burst of aimed fire. The lesson had been drilled into him again and again on battlefields across the globe—gunfights were won with aimed fire.

He pressed himself against a column as bullets chipped the concrete all around him. Flinching, protecting his eyes from the tiny shrapnel and abrasive grit, he looked up at the glass walls and ceiling lining the perimeter of the mall space.

There was just enough of a reflection for him to see, without breaking cover, where the enemy was located. Several of the Padan Muka were grouped together, firing as one, hammering away at the column sheltering him. Perhaps they thought, given time and enough magazines, they could eat their way through the column and get to him. That seemed unlikely, but you never knew.

He judged the angle as best he could, applying everything his experienced sniper's mind had learned over the course of his life on the battlefield. Working backward and half-blind like this, he took his time to do it right.

The muzzle of the M-4 with its underbarrel grenade launcher poked out against the column. Bullets struck all around it, but fortunately did not hit the weapon itself. The soldier took a few last, precious moments to make sure of the trajectory.

The Executioner triggered a grenade.

The 40-mm high-explosive round struck the floor

in front of the knot of Padan Muka killers. The explosion tore through them, scattering them, blowing out the glass wall behind them. Shards of glass and pieces of men flew through the gaping hole in the side of the mall, whipped about by winds outside the multistory building.

Bolan took advantage of the chaos to reload the rifle and the grenade launcher, immediately triggering a second blast in the direction of the fleeing, confused Padan Muka gunners. The explosion blew a second hole in the side of the building, taking out a portion of column that threw chunks of reinforced concrete into the ranks of the killers.

Bolan was not merely wreaking chaos for the sake of chaos. He was consciously angling his fire and maneuvering toward the enemy in a fashion that drove the Padan Muka farther away from Jawan and Rosli. With luck, the heavy kiosk would protect both of them from stray bullets and shrapnel. The rest was up to Bolan.

He moved among the Padan Muka, gliding heel-and-toe, his body a fluid, stable firing platform from which he directed withering, relentless, merciless blasts of 5.56-mm standard ammunition. In some corner of his brain, the mental counter he kept of the predators he eliminated was slowly, inexorably rising, killer by killer, thug by thug.

The Padan Muka were no better than the BR. Their ranks were made of men who were predators. They brutalized. They abused. They violated. They misused those weaker than they, because they could. They took what they wanted and they did not care who was injured or killed.

Worse, the Padan Muka were secret police—the mechanism of oppression in dictatorial regimes the world over. They were the foot soldiers of Fahzal's will, the enforcers of Fahzal's wrongs. They were the muscle behind the threats; they were the means through which the ends were achieved.

The Executioner had taken on a lot of criminals in his endless war. He had fought every kind of predator that walked the Earth, from street punks to drug dealers, mob bosses to corrupt politicians, madmen to terrorists. By far the ones with the most blood on their hands were goons like these—men who followed any order, no matter how immoral, who in turn indulged their baser, animal desires as they stumbled through life committing acts of abuse and degradation.

With the M-4 pressed against his shoulder, Bolan fired round after round. He switched to single shots to mop up, moving through the debris and smoke his grenades had created. The Padan Muka's lines were broken; they were coughing, struggling, wounded; their spirits had been crushed. The combat initiative was Bolan's entirely. He had taken it from them, had turned their world upside down, and was systematically, methodically, ruthlessly ending the threat they represented.

And then, finally, there were no more of them.

Bolan stopped and reloaded, his head swiveling to assess his combat environment.

"Rosli?" he shouted.

"Here!"

"Status!"

"We are fine," Rosli shouted back. "No injuries."

"I'm coming in," Bolan warned.

He found Rosli and Jawan covered in debris and dust, but otherwise unharmed. The CIA operative brushed the boy off as best he could, careful to remove small pebbles of glass that seemed to cover every surface. As

Rosli and Jawan climbed out from behind the kiosk, Jawan looked around in amazement.

"You have certainly done your usual thorough work here," Rosli said.

"We're not done yet," Bolan replied. "Rosli, where would Fahzal likely be, about now?"

"Either seeing to the government or perhaps overseeing his operations in the ghetto." Rosli shrugged. "I am informed that he spends the majority of his time at his offices in Putrajaya."

"Where is that?"

Rosli explained, briefly, the framework of Malaysian government, including the locations of the halls of power and the prime minister's home. As he did so, he started to look more and more alarmed.

"Uh…Cooper…you are not contemplating what I think you are contemplating, are you?"

Bolan looked at him.

"You cannot be serious," Rosli said.

"Deadly serious," Bolan said.

"Just so," Rosli added. "But what you contemplate is practically suicide."

"Maybe. Maybe not. Can you get Jawan somewhere safe?"

"Yes," Rosli said. "But are you sure you do not want my help?"

"I'll have to do without." Bolan shook his head. "We need to make sure Jawan's out of danger. When I'm done with Fahzal, this should all be over."

Rosli extended his hand. Bolan took it. The two men shook, and Rosli smiled at the big American.

"You are like no other government agent I have ever worked with," Rosli said. "It has been an…enlightening experience, Mr. Cooper."

"You've done a damned good job yourself, Rosli," Bolan told him. "Watch your back. Take care of the boy. And take the rifle. You obviously know how to use it."

"I will do so," Rosli said.

Bolan knelt and looked at Jawan. "Rosli's going to look after you. It's going to be okay, Jawan. I know it's been difficult for you, but things will get easier from here on out."

"You're…not going to kill my father, are you?" Jawan asked, swallowing hard.

Bolan looked at him with sorrow. "No, Jawan. I'm not going to kill your father. That's a promise."

Rosli threw Bolan his car keys. "Take the car," he said. "I can get another."

"Thanks," Bolan said. "Goodbye, Rosli."

"Goodbye, Mr. Cooper. Good luck to you."

"And to you."

With that, Bolan left, once more marching forward, toward danger.

15

Putrajaya, Bolan knew, became the new capital of Malaysia in the late 1990s, replacing overcrowded Kuala Lumpur as the seat of Malaysia's federal government. A planned city, Putrajaya boasted much greenery and many beautiful gardens, as well as a variety of tourist attractions and a population in the tens of thousands.

The office of the prime minister was an imposing structure known as Perdana Putra. Overlooking the Dataran Putra, the beginning of the Putra Boulevard, it sat on the lakeshore and boasted impressive Muslim architectural flourishes. The central, onion-shaped dome was flanked by smaller minarets, the green of the domes resplendent against the blue sky.

There was security, but it was designed to prevent wholesale military action. Bolan was one man, easily missed. He strode directly to the security station before the complex, pausing to wait while the guard on duty looked up from his clipboard.

The guard said something in Malaysian.

"Matthew Cooper to see the prime minister," Bolan said.

The guard looked up, his eyes widening.

Bolan punched him in the face, hard. The guard went down like a prizefighter with a glass jaw.

The Executioner stepped past the security checkpoint.

He had consulted with the Farm using his satellite phone, while driving to Putrajaya. According to Price's team, the majority of the security deployed to protect Fahzal would be inside the office complex, and it would be comprised of Padan Muka. That was fine by Bolan. While he did not relish the thought of removing from his way guards who were simply loyal to their government and its leadership, the idea of taking on the Padan Muka once more was something he welcomed.

He'd had enough of Fahzal and his schemes. He'd had enough of the man's murderous legions of private troops. He'd had enough of racism and hatred posing as government policy. He had looked back on the path of dead bodies in his wake and been more indignant than ever at the actions of societal predators like Fahzal and his goons, who, in their greed and their power lust, in their wanton desire to gratify themselves at any cost, exacted an unconscionable toll in human life on the very populations they were supposed to represent and protect.

It was the problem of the world, the reason that war occurred and men like Mack Bolan were needed on the battlegrounds of those wars. Fahzal and his government were, collectively, everything that was wrong with global politics and socioeconomics. Fahzal would never understand that, at least not on his own.

Bolan intended to explain it to him.

Personally.

He gave up all pretense of being a lone tourist as he pushed through the wide doors leading him inside the government complex. His pistols came out from under his shirt as he stalked forward, grim determination on his face.

He knew there would be a few innocents—government employees and perhaps even tourists who had nothing to do with the battle he was about to wage. He would, as he always did, shield them from the effects of his war. No innocents would die by Bolan's hand, nor through his negligence.

Someone saw him with his guns out and screamed in fear. Bolan ignored that. The Farm had transmitted to him a floor layout of the office complex. He had memorized the route he would need to take to get to the prime minister's suite of offices. No one and nothing was going to stop him. He was going to have a word with Prime Minister Fahzal, in person, directly.

He heard rapid footsteps. Moving to put himself against the wall of the corridor, he started shouting at the lingering civilians and government workers. "Everybody out!" he commanded. "Evacuate! Go!" Then he saw the lever for the fire alarm. Smashing the protective glass, he yanked the lever inside. "Fire!" he yelled. "Fire in the building! Everyone out!"

The ringing alarm bells had the desired effect. People started streaming past him, ignoring him or staring at him in fear as they noticed his weapons. It wouldn't matter. It might be that the entire local police department and military descended on this place in reaction, but that, too, did not matter. For the moment, all Bolan needed to do was get the innocents out of harm's way.

Then it would just be him and the Padan Muka.

The first wave of brown-and-black-uniformed thugs charged down the hallway, apparently eager to confront whomever was capable of creating such a disturbance

on their own turf. Bolan, guns in hand, simply waited
for them to come.

The first group carried truncheons, probably because
displays of automatic weaponry in the offices of government were considered bad for tourism.

Bolan waited for the suicidal charge that seemed to
be the hallmark of the Padan Muka. As the first man
swung his club, Bolan shot him.

He fired again. And again. And again. He pumped
bullets into each man, dropping them in turn, sprawling
them in the hallway in a crumpled mess.

He kept walking.

The next Padan Muka guards were smarter. They
had Uzi submachine guns and they started firing from
the shelter of the doorways at the end of the corridor.

The big American increased his pace. As the bullets tore the floor around and behind him, he ran faster
and faster. Finally, he threw himself to the floor, his
arms extended. As he skidded across the floor thanks
to the momentum he had built, he fired his guns, killing
each man as he passed, his aim infallible and his will
unwavering.

Then he got up, and he kept walking.

Another group of Padan Muka attacked him from
above as he took the stairs to the next floor. He paused,
waited for them to overextend themselves and then
started picking them off one by one with precise head
shots. Each dead man toppled like a stone, falling
through the stairwell opening and crashing to the floor
below.

Bolan was in the zone now. He continued to fire,
dropping magazines from each gun in turn, reloading
as he went.

Then he ran out of ammunition.

Bolan's Desert Eagle and Beretta fired empty. He reached into the canvas messenger bag for spares and there were none.

The only weapon available was the Makarov pistol he had taken earlier, which he'd placed inside the bag after recovering his weapons in Jelel's hotel room. He checked the small pistol, which was loaded with seven rounds, and tucked it into his waistband over his appendix.

The door to the prime minister's office loomed before him. He dropped his empty guns into the war bag and placed the bag on the floor.

There was a very pretty young receptionist or clerk of some kind in the outer office. Bolan ignored her and continued to the inner rooms. He tried the heavy wooden door, but it was locked. Undeterred, he kicked it in.

Two men waited inside.

Bolan recognized the one seated behind the desk. Fahzal looked terrified, his forehead beaded with sweat. He wore an expensive, tailored business suit and he held a small pocket pistol in his hand.

"At last, you are here—" Fahzal started.

Bolan didn't wait for the inevitable speech. The men who masterminded these grand schemes always seemed to want to talk about them, when finally confronted, and Bolan wasn't in the mood. With lightning-fast reflexes, he drew the loaded, chambered Makarov and fired a single round into the top of Fahzal's desk. The round passed through Fahzal's palm to get there. The prime minister shrieked in pain, his hand spraying blood around the room.

That roused the very large man standing behind the desk. Bolan didn't know this one, but soon had a name to put with the dull features.

"Majid!" Fahzal screamed. "Kill him!"

Bolan adjusted his aim, ready to pump a round into the big Malaysian, but the large man was deceptively fast. He tackled Bolan with a bear hug that was meant, quite literally, to squeeze the life from the soldier's lungs. Bolan hit the floor with Majid on top of him, his lungs on fire and his ribs cracking. He lost the pistol.

Bolan felt the large man moving for position. Majid began swinging his huge fists, slamming his knuckles into Bolan's jaw with numbing power. Bolan reeled under the assault. The big Malaysian was much heavier and clearly very skilled in his ground game. Bolan knew, as sure as he knew the big man was punching him, that if he didn't change position and do something very quickly, the Malaysian was going to beat him to death.

He raised his arms, trying to get his fingers into Majid's face. The big man laughed, obviously expecting that, and wrapped his arms around Bolan more tightly, compressing Bolan's ribs while pinning his arms to his body. Bolan could feel the big man's rancid breath on his face as Majid started laughing, the basso rumble disturbing and bizarre all at once. Here was a man who enjoyed killing, most assuredly.

With no weapons available to him, Bolan used his chin, jamming it into Majid's eye socket and grinding it in for all he was worth.

Majid roared in pain and outrage. His grip slackened just enough; Bolan was able to wrench his arms free. He boxed both of Majid's ears, cupping his palms and slapping the man's ears as hard as he possibly could. When the Malaysian screamed, Bolan got one leg under himself and, while his opponent was distracted, rolled both of them over. With Majid beneath him, he wrapped his fingers around the man's face and pressed his thumbs against the big man's closed eyes with every ounce of his strength.

The sound that erupted from Majid's lips was almost inhuman. In a burst of pain, rage and adrenaline, he surged to his feet, throwing Bolan across the room and against the desk. Blind and enraged beyond the limits of sanity, Majid stumbled forward, his big, knobby fists clenching and unclenching.

He grabbed the prime minister by mistake.

"No! No, you fool! Not me! Not me!" Fahzal shouted.

Majid began twisting. He looked as if he might rend Fahzal limb from limb. Blood streamed from his face and he roared his fury. It was like something from a monster movie.

Bolan's hand fell on something cold and hard on the floor. It was the prime minister's little pocket pistol. Bolan grabbed the gun, pointed it and started pulling the trigger.

He had no choice; he was forced to shoot Majid in the back. He emptied the little gun's magazine, trying to kill the big Malaysian before he could murder the prime minister. The little gun clicked empty and Bolan let it fall, prepared to leap forward and start stabbing his enormous foe.

Fahzal fell from the big man's grasp. He hit the floor hard, gasping and wheezing, and looked up at Majid in abject horror. Majid began to sway back and forth. Finally, his brain at last got the message his body was trying to send to it. He toppled like a felled tree, going rigid and slamming into the floor with such force that books on the shelves in Fahzal's office vibrated from the impact.

The Executioner checked Majid's pulse. The man was dead.

Bolan grabbed Fahzal, lifted him bodily and threw him into the chair behind his desk. "Call off your thugs," he said to Fahzal. "I see one more Padan Muka goon within a hundred yards, and I'll finish the job your boy Majid started."

Fahzal pressed a button. His door swung shut automatically, moving on hydraulic hinges of some kind. When the locks had clicked into place, he pressed a button on his intercom. Bolan could hear Fahzal's voice echoing through the corridors of the administration complex.

"This is Prime Minister Fahzal," he said hoarsely. "Padan Muka, stand down. I repeat, you are to stand down. Take no action. Do not come to my office. This is an order. You will obey it." He turned the intercom off. Then he looked up at Bolan, who had recovered his fallen Makarov and was pointing it at the prime minister.

"Good," Bolan said. "Now, I want you to call off the ghetto raids."

Fahzal looked at him. "But my son—"

"Your son is fine," Bolan said. "He's safe. No thanks to the Padan Muka, who are trying to kill him."

"What? That is ridiculous. My men would never try to kill my son."

"Do you mean to tell me you didn't order it?"

"What is this nonsense?" Fahzal seemed genuinely outraged. "I would never order the death of my son! I would never endanger my boy…"

Bolan realized now what had been bothering him all along. "But you would," he said finally. "And you did. It was all your idea, wasn't it? You tipped the BR and made sure they'd take your son. And you had the Padan Muka arrange to kill him when it looked like you'd get him back too early."

"No!" Fahzal said desperately.

Bolan pressed the muzzle of the compact Makarov to Fahzal's forehead. "If you're going to lie to me," Bolan said, "I'm afraid our conversation won't be terribly productive."

"All right!" Fahzal shouted. "All right! I did use poor Jawan, to some degree. But Nasir assured me that he would be safe! He said the BR would not harm Jawan as long as they thought he could be used to get to me!"

"Nasir. That would be Nasir, your head of security? Leader of the Padan Muka?"

"Yes." Fahzal nodded. "I…what did you say about the Padan Muka?"

"I said the Padan Muka tried to kill your boy, Fahzal," Bolan said. "Tell me, if that order was given and it wasn't given by you, who *would* have told them to do it?"

"It could only have been Nasir."

"And why would Nasir do that?" Bolan asked. "Perhaps because he knew if you got Jawan back before the assault on the ghetto, before you were ready to carry out your genocidal plans, that public support for the attack might wane?"

"That is insane," Fahzal said, sounding very confused.

"You don't believe me?" Bolan asked. "Where is he? Find him. Tell him. Tell him you know everything. See if he doesn't admit it."

Fahzal looked at Bolan and then to the phone on his desk. He picked up the receiver and dialed a number from memory. He put the phone on speaker.

"Nasir. This is Fahzal."

"Yes, Prime Minister? I am pleased to report that we are almost ready to commence the final phase of the solution to our ghetto problem."

"Nasir…I know," Fahzal said.

"I do not understand," Nasir said. "You know what, exactly?"

"I know what you did," Fahzal said. "I know you intended to kill my son. For your own reasons."

There was a long silence. Finally, Nasir said, "Well. You would have figured it out yourself sooner or later. I suppose there is no harm in you knowing now."

"But…my son!" Fahzal said.

"Yes, yes, I have heard about nothing else for days now," Nasir said dismissively. "I am sick to death of it, to be honest. He is but a boy. He is expendable. You have how many mistresses? You could make another without even trying."

Bolan gestured with the Makarov.

"Enough, Nasir!" Fahzal said, looking at Bolan and then back to the phone. "You will call off the entire operation. You will do it now. Withdraw everyone. The Padan Muka is to stand down."

Nasir paused.

"No," he said finally.

"What?" Fahzal demanded. "How dare you defy me? I am your prime minister!"

"And who do you think put you in that office?" Nasir asked. "Fahzal, I am sorry you are having trouble with the reality of the situation, but the fact is, Jawan would have been of much more use to us dead. Certainly of more use than he or your other offspring have ever been to us alive. But no matter. What is done or not done, well, it does not matter. I am going to burn out this scourge on our nation, Fahzal, and I am going to do it because it is necessary. You can cooperate and benefit, or you can oppose me and die. Either way, I am done listening to you bark." The last words were full of contempt.

The speaker switched to a loud dial tone.

Stunned, Fahzal sat back heavily in his chair. He looked to Bolan. "I…I cannot believe he has done this. I cannot believe how he has used me."

"Yeah," Bolan said. "Your kind never does."

Fahzal said nothing. Finally, he looked up again. "I cannot call off the ghetto raid. He refuses."

"Then we'll have to do it the old-fashioned way. Have you got a helicopter and a pilot here?"

"Yes," Fahzal said. "I have this. Why?"

"Because we're sharing a cab," Bolan said, "and you're paying the driver."

16

Nasir stood on the back of the jeep, which had a belt-fed RPK light machine gun on a mount in the back. He was surrounded by Padan Muka forces, some with Kalashnikovs, some with flamethrowers.

He thought it was a beautiful sight.

His moment of triumph should have been total, and in truth, very little would sway him from his course of action. But the call from the prime minister had irritated him. Fahzal had a lot of nerve, finding his spine only now, presuming to tell him how to run an operation of this scale. Imagine that—call off the raid? Nonsense! After all the time, the resources, the energy spent in making arrangements. After all the bloody fighting with this CIA madman who had vexed them thus far, this madman who, as far as Nasir knew, was still at large.

He had tried and failed to gauge the amount of death and destruction caused by one man—or one man and that idiot Rosli, whom the BR, the rebels and Fahzal's regime all knew was a CIA "covert" asset. Nasir still could not figure out how, when he had first gotten word that the CIA was bringing in a Western troubleshooter to intervene in the hostage crisis, his Padan Muka had been unable to kill this lone warrior. Yes, the Americans often produced very skilled fighters, but he was *one man*. It made no sense that one man had slaughtered so many Padan Muka fighters—and an equal or greater number of BR terrorists, as well! What manner of monster was the American government producing?

He looked forward to a day when Malaysia was powerful enough and influential enough to challenge America and the West more directly. They would not have to put up with the United States' arrogant interference for very much longer. The destruction of this common foe, and the support that it was helping to generate for the Nationalist Party of Malaysia, was only the beginning of Nasir's grand plan to make Malaysia the crown jewel of Southeast Asia.

Fahzal's sudden desire to spare the rebels and the subnormal race contributing to the rebels' ranks left a sour taste in Nasir's mouth. It was as if he had tasted the fruit of victory, only to have Fahzal try to snatch it from his mouth. He would be damned if he would give it up; a victory swallowed in haste, while not as savory as a victory one could truly enjoy, was still success. It was still of benefit.

Even more annoying was the fact that he could not raise Majid. He had tried both phone and radio and could not reach his field lieutenant in any way. Of all the people who should be here at this moment, the moment of the triumphant raid on the ghetto and those festering within it, he could think of no one more appropriate than Majid. Where was he?

Nasir sighed. He supposed it did not matter. He would not let Fahzal's weakness ruin this moment. He did not intend to let Majid's less than total reliability ruin it, either. Perhaps the big man had found himself a rare, willing woman and was too busy with that to notice he was being sought. He would turn up eventually. After all, it was not as if Majid were going to get into a fight in some downtown bar and then lose. Majid was a force of nature, a lion among sheep.

That made Nasir the lion tamer, which was fine with him.

Fahzal did not matter. Majid's absence did not matter. Only that Nasir was in power, and Nasir would continue to be in power, and those Nasir knew to be inferior were about to be removed. The cancer that infected Malaysia was about to be cut out and, while the operation would cause the patient pain, that patient would go on to be healthy and strong because of it.

"First wave," he ordered into his walkie-talkie. "Advance!"

The men with the flamethrowers advanced, walking in tandem with one assault-rifle-wielding Padan Muka fighter each. Nasir had devised this strategy himself, and he was very proud of it. He might, he thought, one day write a book about it. It might be the case that, with the passage of time, history would come to recognize him as the great man he truly was. He could but hope so. He knew that right now, feelings were too raw and there were those who, in their weakness, would not understand the extreme measures to which it was necessary for him to turn. He could understand that. He could be generous about it. It was, after all, only natural that men like Nasir, men who could make these hard decisions, were misunderstood by their lessers.

He watched through a pair of field glasses, standing on the back of the jeep like the conquering hero he knew himself to be. The glasses provided excellent clarity and detail. As one of his men grabbed a civilian woman and began tearing her clothes off, dragging her into one of the nearby shanty huts, Nasir had an excellent view. He had most assuredly indulged himself with female ghetto prisoners many times in the past day. They were inferior human beings, but that did not mean they did not have their uses. He supposed, if any survived the destruction, he might have some taken back to his office in the prime minister's complex. It would amuse him to have one of them handcuffed under his desk. The thought made him chuckle.

As he watched, the first flamethrower-men reached their targets. The units on their backs projected bright streams of liquid flame at the outermost fringes of the shantytown. The corrugated metal would not burn, but the tarps, the plywood, the blankets, the garbage and the people would all burn.

He would burn it all clean. Burn it all until the cancer was cured.

His phone began to ring.

"Yes?"

"Nasir…" Fahzal's voice was distorted. "You must stop this."

"I can barely hear you," Nasir said, annoyed. "Is that… Are you in your helicopter? I have told you not to call me from that damnable thing. I can understand almost nothing you say when you are in the air."

"Nasir," Fahzal said, doing his best to make himself heard. "You need to stop this! The climate has changed. We dare not take this action now."

"You are simply upset, old friend," Nasir said, coaxing the prime minister as he had successfully so many times before. It was not true, after all, that Fahzal had no will of his own. He was easily enough nettled, and when upset, he could be a very real obstacle. Several times during their career together, Fahzal had gotten it into his head that he needed to assert his authority, to prove that he lived in no one's shadow and under no one's thumb. When that happened, Nasir knew from experience, it took a fair amount of flattery to placate him. The mood would pass, though. It always had before.

"I am not simply upset!" Fahzal said. "Do you not realize that the plan is going wrong?"

"The plan has been perfect," Nasir said. "Perfect in every way, in that it has worked. Yes, certain things have not gone exactly as we expected, but that is always the way. Grow up, Fahzal! The world is complicated and messy. We cannot predict everything. We can only plan for contingencies and be flexible enough to adapt to them. We have done this! You have nothing to complain about."

"If you conduct these raids, the people will rise up! I will be unseated!"

"That is nonsense," Nasir said. "You knew when we started that we would build the necessary public support. It started by making the people aware of the nature of the lesser races among them. It continued by layering on public policies that reinforced the inferiority of those races. Pressure here. A push there. A bit of influence over there. Suddenly, the inferiors have been forced, by policy and by regulation and by public opinion, to remain in only those neighborhoods allowed them."

"But—"

"Do not interrupt me, Fahzal," Nasir said. "We moved the Indians and the Chinese into this place. We watched as they continued to multiply, to rot here, their fetid, miserable, teeming masses growing a bigger blight on our society every day. Our agents encouraged BR, encouraged them to grow more bold. We made sure that BR knew where to put its hands on your son, and we encouraged them to believe, at every possible turn, that you were the author of their oppression. We gave them just enough information to turn your son's school into the worst act of terrorism on Malaysian soil to date. And our people recoiled in horror as we explained to them the nature of BR, of the rebels, of the Indian and Chinese subraces living among them. It was the perfect plan, Fahzal."

"You do not understand! The Americans—"

"Yes, yes," Fahzal said. "The Americans. The ever-interfering Americans. Well, they sent us their murderous bastard, and he is still out there somewhere. But we will deal with him. At least he has spared us hunting down BR, now that they have served their purpose. They would have persisted, after all, even after their population base was largely destroyed or expelled from our land. Face it, Fahzal. We are about to achieve our dreams. Our plans are about to come to fruition. We are triumphant. All that remains is burning out the filth in our midst. Now, wherever it is you are flying, go there and leave me be. Hide if you must. I will find you when the people require a public address, and not before. Remember which of us truly runs things, and do not forget it."

Nasir closed the phone and put it in his pocket, disgusted at Fahzal's weak will. He cocked his head to one side then. He could have sworn he'd heard a helicopter. That was not possible, however; Fahzal was very uncomfortable near the ghetto. He would not fly there voluntarily. The airspace around the ghetto was supposed to be a no-fly zone, however. When the operation was over he would have to check with the nearest airport and find out if someone had violated government policy. He would have whoever was responsible executed for this breach.

He returned to watching the operation.

The men with the assault rifles were there to cover the flamethrower operators. The rebels had become increasingly organized. Possibly the denizens of the ghetto understood, on some instinctive if not explicit level, that they would all be killed. No human being, when forced into containment of this type, does not think of that possibility, if conditions persist. Frankly he thought it a testament to their inferiority that they had ever allowed themselves to be so corralled.

That made him chuckle. He saw no reason he should wish for more worthy adversaries, after all; he enjoyed an easy victory. But there were times when one couldn't help but wonder how it was that an entire people would allow itself to be slaughtered. It was just more proof of their weakness, as Nasir saw it.

The riflemen began firing on full-automatic. Rebels were approaching in large groups, moving up the street formed by two rows of makeshift shacks nearest the Padan Muka troops' position. Nasir stomped his foot three times, the signal to his driver to start the engine and relocate the jeep.

His driver obediently fired the engine and brought them closer to the main part of the action. From where he was parked, he had a good field of fire over the heads of his Padan Muka fighters. He almost tripped over an entrenching tool loose in the back of the jeep; he kicked it aside. Bracing himself, he pulled back the bolt of the belt-fed RPK, allowing his field glasses to fall to the end of their strap around his neck.

The rebels were using rocks, a few firearms—including some captured Kalashnikovs—and Molotov cocktails. As Nasir watched, a firebomb exploded near the Padan Muka lines. One of the men caught fire, running and screaming, his clothes coated in whatever sticky fuel the rebels were using in their bombs. The head of the Padan Muka observed, completely captivated, as the man burned to death, rolling around in agony.

The troopers were firing in earnest now, eager to prevent that fate from befalling them. Some of the rebels were killed outright. Others were wounded. Still others withdrew, trying to drag a few of the wounded with them to safety. The Padan Muka, enraged by the deadly resistance, began firing into the wounded, then into those who tried to carry them.

Nasir leaned into the RPK and, laughing, added its heavy bullets to the chaos. He tracked left, then right, blowing apart fresh corpses and fleeing rebels alike. There was something to be said for taking a direct involvement in your work, Nasir thought to himself. It felt good. It felt just.

A good battle plan had to be complex enough to work, but simple enough to be adaptable and understandable. He knew that much.

His Kalashnikov-wielding troops would cover the flamethrower-men as the flame units advanced, burning each layer of the ghetto in turn. It was going to take time; such a process could be nothing but almost excruciatingly slow. As they burned each layer, however, the riflemen would be able to mop up any rebels and civilians who had survived the fire. They would kill any active rebels and also any wounded survivors, then move up and allow the flamethrower-men to repeat the process.

Nasir had many more jeeps like the one in which he

rode. Fire teams would use those jeeps to drive through
the charred wreckage, their machine guns put to good
use making sure that nothing moved and nothing continued to live. No survivors meant no witnesses. Fahzal's
forces had taken state control of the nation's media out-
lets upon Fahzal's rise to power; no word of what happened would leak out. Once he brought in public-works
crews to bulldoze the ashes and begin erecting government housing and other planned municipal projects, it
would be as if the Indians, the Chinese, their miserable
subrace of Malaysians and their ghetto never existed. In
this way, Nasir was rewriting history.

It was almost like having the powers of a god. Just
thinking that gave Nasir a thrill. Was he not the most
powerful man in all of Southeast Asia? Given time for
Malaysia to grow and develop, to prosper as the corrupt
industrial nations of the West had developed, and Nasir
might himself one day be the most powerful man in all
the world.

That was a long way off yet. But it was possible.

Nasir watched as several more of his men fired their
weapons into storming crowds of rebels. The ghetto
denizens were becoming desperate. They had seen the
smoke and the flames. They had seen the fiery fate that
awaited them. Like cornered animals, they were lashing
out, and their desperation made them very dangerous.

Once more he wished Majid were there to enjoy the
scene. The big man would be very upset that he was
missing the big raid, the culmination of all the Padan
Muka's efforts.

The outer layers of the ghetto were roiling with smoke
and flame. His Padan Muka riflemen were shooting
many rebels and encountering diminishing resistance,

so it was time to implement the last phase of his plan. He keyed his walkie-talkie again.

"Snipers," he said. "This is Nasir. Begin your work. Do not stop until you run out of ammunition or targets."

"Understood, sir," came the replies.

The cracks of the big sniper rifles, firing from atop the church and other high points at the fringes of the ghetto, began to echo down to the Padan Muka on the ground. The sound emboldened his men, for it was the sound of death from the skies, the sound of superiority from the high ground. In areas of the ghetto too far away for even Nasir with his field glasses to see, ghetto residents would be falling, dead, while their fellow scum screamed and cried and bemoaned this new and unjust fate.

The thought made him smile. They would never know what hit them.

He listened to the periodic explosions from high above, the sound almost pleasant to his ears. He tried to picture the people the heavy sniper rifles were removing from this earth. He envied the snipers their vantage and the powerful telescopic sights through which they viewed those whose lives they claimed.

When he had judged that this had gone on long enough, he took up the walkie-talkie again.

"This is Nasir," he said into the device. "We have done very well. We will continue to bring the fight to the enemy. We will continue to remove this scourge from our soil. All units, move forward. Flamethrowers, next row of structures. Rifles, be alert, and remember, we have much, much more ammunition stockpiled. Do not save it! Use it, and make your Malaysia a safe place for Malaysians! Do it for your families! Do it for your country!"

A cheer rose up among the Padan Muka. Nasir keyed the walkie-talkie off and smiled. They loved him. They dearly and truly loved their leader, and well they should. He was bringing them glory. He was bringing them power. He was bringing them a bright future.

He was a great man, Nasir thought. Yes, truly, he was. The knowledge of it warmed his heart.

"Snipers," Nasir said into his radio. "Let us hear you. I have not heard a shot in some time."

"You got it," came the reply.

To the left of Nasir's jeep, one of his riflemen raised his weapon. The man was tracking a rebel holding a Molotov cocktail.

The rifleman's head exploded.

The thunder of the sniper rifle above sounded, and Nasir realized that something had gone horribly wrong.

"You up there!" he shouted into his radio. "Check your fire!"

"You got it," the voice said again. Another Padan Muka fighter, this one a flamethrower carrier, pitched forward. The sound of the rifle above and behind Nasir's location marked it as more sniper fire. There was a third boom, on the heels of a massive explosion; the sniper had fired into the fallen man's flamethrower pack, and the unit had exploded. Men for dozens of feet in every direction were rolling on the ground, covered in burning fuel they could not shake off.

"You fool!" Nasir shouted. "What are you doing?"

"Just taking out the garbage," said the voice.

Nasir could not know it, but the Executioner had arrived.

17

The Executioner, with the captured sniper rifle pressed against his shoulder, was prone on top of the church tower. The weapon's telescopic sight provided him with a perfect picture of the Padan Muka thugs below. He wore a radio headset taken from the sniper whose throat he had cut. He used the headset to goad Nasir. Something about that just seemed fitting.

Below him, the Padan Muka continued their brutal attack.

Having Fahzal's pilot drop him near the ghetto had been easy enough, and the ride had been fast enough to get him into the action from the prime minister's offices, before it was too late. He had disliked giving Fahzal the chance to let Nasir know he was coming, but there was nothing to be done about it. As soon as Bolan left the chopper, Fahzal might have been on the radio or the phone to his chief of security, warning him of the danger.

What Bolan would not do, however, was kill the man to stop him from talking, and if he wasn't willing to do that, there was nothing to stop Fahzal from interfering. He could have destroyed the radio in the chopper and made sure neither man had a cell phone, but they would simply have found some other means of calling Nasir. He could have tied them both up, too, but to do it properly and make it last would have taken too long.

He told Fahzal's pilot to take off and fly due north until Bolan couldn't see him anymore, if that pilot did not, in fact, want a bullet through the eye.

As he entered the ghetto area on foot, he had quickly determined his next course of action. The church tower had been the most logical vantage for a sniper. When he started hearing the big rifles fire, he knew he would have his choice of equipment. Entering the old church, he had encountered several guards, whom he killed with his knife to prevent being detected. Then he climbed to the top of the tower, snuck up on the two snipers there and killed them both. Finally, he had used one of the captured Dragunovs to find, and shoot, every other sniper within sight of his location. That had the benefit of protecting him from counter sniper fire, while also reducing the ability of the Padan Muka thugs to kill innocents within the ghetto.

Shooting targets on the ground had opened the game in earnest and, of course, alerted Nasir to his presence.

Leaving Nasir to sputter and fume—he reached up and reduced the volume to his headset. When Nasir started screaming into his walkie-talkie, Bolan peered through the telescopic sight and got down to the work he was born to do.

"American," Nasir said, apparently having regained his composure. "American, I know you can hear me."

"I can hear you," Bolan said. He shot a Padan Muka on the ground. Then he shot another.

"Stop!" Nasir shrieked. "You do not know what you are doing! You do not realize what you are ruining!"

"Don't I?" Bolan asked. He started tracking the men with the flamethrower packs. "I think I'm stopping a racist madman from committing genocide by burning a bunch of unarmed civilians to death. Or did I misunderstand?"

"But there is a higher purpose here," Nasir almost whined. "We are making a better Malaysia!"

"Somehow I doubt most of your countrymen think that," Bolan said. He drew in a breath, let it out slowly and held half of it. Then he fired.

A man with a flamethrower pack exploded. Bolan had targeted the pressure valve on the rear of the flamethrower pack, which had caused an impressive detonation. He began slowly tracking from left to right across the full field of fire below him, shooting men with flamethrowers by preference. Each time one of them exploded, the flames covered a lot of ground. Padan Muka guards were burned or burning, running and screaming as they tried to put out their clothing, their skin, their hair.

Bolan kept up the pressure.

He had plenty of spare loaded magazines for his captured rifle. The Padan Muka had evidently settled in for a long, deadly siege, and they had come prepared. Well, that was okay. He would put their cache to good use, turning it against them. He found another man with a flamethrower in the crosshairs of his rifle. A press of the weapon's trigger and the man was a staggering roman candle.

Bolan kept shooting. He shot men with rifles. He shot men with flamethrowers. He shot several men driving trucks with mounted belt-fed machine guns, punching the rifle rounds through the light sheet metal of the jeeps they drove. With each explosion, with each new bullet in the head of a Padan Muka thug, Nasir's screams intensified. Bolan had to turn down his radio twice more, though he did not silence Nasir completely. Driving his enemy into incoherent rage was part of his plan. He needed Nasir off balance. Watching his elaborate plan for the ghetto quite literally explode around his ears was doing that job. Bolan intended to make him pay in excruciating detail for every man, woman and child that the Padan Muka had hurt.

"Please, American," Nasir begged. "We can work together. You are perhaps a mercenary? We can pay. I have access to vast funds. Fahzal's government has the resources to employ one such as you. Think of what we could accomplish! You would hold a high rank in our organization, something commensurate with your ability."

"Nasir," Bolan said, unable to help himself. "Did I at any point give you the impression that I was stupid?"

"I do not know what you mean," Nasir said, sounding genuinely confused.

"We both know," Bolan said, "that you're not going to forget how I've humiliated you. Your kind never forgives that sort of thing. You'll promise me whatever I want and then shoot or stab me in the back just as soon as you have the opportunity."

Nasir began screaming furiously in his native language.

Bolan ignored that. He continued raining death on the ground below.

The afternoon light was waning. The fires below were growing much larger, brighter and hotter, and they were starting to spread across the debris and among the clothing of the many dead men below. The flames were starting to creep closer to the church, threatening to surround Bolan and everyone else in the ghetto.

Bolan paused to retrieve his secure satellite phone. He dialed the Farm and waited.

"Price," Stony Man's mission controller said.

"Barb," Bolan said, "Striker. I'm afraid I've started quite a fire. Has Bear had any luck with the contingency I mentioned when we last spoke?"

"He has," Price said. "We've been tracking the situation using thermal imaging from one of the NSA's spy satellites, too. We can see the fires growing. You'll be pleased to know that the larger fire control outfits in the city are computer dispatched. Bear has hacked the dispatcher system and is making sure that fire trucks and firefighters are on their way to you. They'll get everything under control."

"Good," Bolan said. "There's not much point saving the ghetto from the Padan Muka if we're just going to burn it down anyway."

"We're on it, Striker."

"Good. Striker out."

The Executioner bent to his work once more.

He fired into the target-rich environment below without bothering to be very selective. There were so many Padan Muka troops that killing one was much like killing another. The chaos and the deaths were having a cumulative effect. Already, some of the Padan Muka soldiers were choosing to flee rather than stay and risk death at the hands of this faceless enemy. That was good. Any amount of fear that broke their ranks was useful to Bolan. A thug who was concerned with saving his own life, who was living with the very real fear that he could be killed at any moment, suddenly lost interest in victimizing others. For creatures of this type, self-preservation wasn't the primary law; it was the only law.

The roaring fires below gave the ghetto a hellish, flickering orange cast. It was like something from an artist's conception of hell. Bolan knew that that wasn't far from the truth. Men like Nasir sought to create hell on Earth, in the name of creating paradise. They inevitably failed; the question was how many victims such men would be allowed to take with them.

There would be no more, if Bolan had anything to say about it.

So intent was he on waging his sniper's war of justice that he almost did not hear the figure approaching from the ladder leading to the bell tower's flat roof. He turned, bringing the rifle up across his chest, just in time to stop the thin blade of the entrenching tool from slamming into the back of his skull. The rifle took the shovel head instead, vibrating in Bolan's hands.

Nasir screamed and brought the shovel up again. He swung with all his might, slamming the makeshift weapon into the roof, taking huge gouges from the tiles.

Bolan tried to bring the Dragunov to bear in order to shoot Nasir, but the distance was wrong. Nasir grabbed the barrel and pulled the weapon past his body. He swung the entrenching tool at Bolan's head, spinning it over his head like a helicopter blade.

"You miserable son of a whore!" he screamed, slashing and slashing over and over again. "I will chop you into the tiniest of pieces and feed you to animals! You have ruined everything! You stupid, interfering Americans and your ridiculous Western ways! You can never leave us to run our own affairs! You have to meddle!

You have to manipulate! I will torture you until you beg to be put to death, and then I will torture you still until you go insane from it!"

The whole time he was talking, Nasir was swinging the entrenching tool, hyperventilating with rage as he screamed his fury.

At least Bolan had succeeded in that much. He had wanted to provoke unreasoning fury in Nasir, and he had. That was good, because otherwise the man might simply have shot him in the back. It was bad enough to take a shovel between the shoulder blades. He wouldn't have been able to stop a bullet fired from across the roof.

Nasir shoved, then pulled the rifle, managing to rip it free and throw it off the roof. There was another weapon on the roof with the other dead sniper's body, but Nasir was between it and Bolan. The other guns were empty and therefore of no use. He had the Makarov tucked into his belt, but the range was too close.

He tried anyway.

He waited for Nasir to lunge with the shovel. When the deranged security chief got close enough, Bolan kicked him, hard. That gave him the space to draw his Makarov and attempt to fire from retention. His finger squeezed the trigger—

Nasir threw himself into Bolan and the both of them almost went off the roof. At the last moment, dropping the pistol, Bolan managed to grab one of the roof tiles, barely hanging on as the two of them grappled right at the edge. Nasir had managed to retain the small shovel and now brought it up, swinging it like a tomahawk over his shoulder. The blade of the tool ripped into the roof of the bell tower, inches from where Bolan's face had been a moment previously.

"You will beg for mercy!" Nasir shouted, hacking away with the shovel. "I will find all of your loved ones and I will make you watch as I mutilate and rape them! I will sell your mother, your wife, your daughters into slavery in a Burmese whorehouse! I will—"

Bolan slammed the heel of his palm up under Nasir's chin, snapping the man's head back and throwing him off balance. The Executioner bucked him off, slamming his boot into his stomach for good measure in a brutal side kick.

"Shut up," Bolan said simply.

Nasir rose, shovel still in hand. Bolan shot to his feet and squared off against the man. The fires raged below.

Bolan threw a toe kick square into Nasir's groin.

The kick was a hard one. It lifted Nasir up off his feet. The entrenching tool went flying over the edge. Nasir himself collapsed on his hands and knees, retching violently. Bolan circled and, never one to give a dangerous adversary quarter before the fight was settled, slammed one booted foot into Nasir's ribs, knocking him over.

He could have railed against Nasir as Nasir had to him. He could have accused the security chief, rightly, of all manner of crimes against humanity. He could have condemned him, excoriated him, indicted him. He could have held him aloft for his Padan Muka thugs to see, then thrown him to his death with righteous glee.

He didn't.

He was the Executioner. He was not a madman. He did what he did to protect the innocent. He was an instrument of justice.

So he simply kicked Nasir in the groin again.

It was time to end things. Bolan waded into the security chief, hammering away with closed-fist blows to his torso and open-hand palm strikes to his head. He knocked the Malaysian around like a speed bag, bruising and breaking and practically deconstructing the man. Finally, he slammed a side kick into one of Nasir's knees. There was a hideous *crack* as something gave. Nasir screamed and collapsed onto the roof of the bell tower.

Bolan stood over his foe breathing heavily.

Nasir was not particularly large or strong. He had no special martial-arts skills. Yet he had been one of the Executioner's more difficult opponents in a hand-to-hand battle. Nasir was proof that force of will counted for much…and that when a man's heart was full of hate and evil, it gave him real power.

Bolan drew in a haggard breath. Nasir was unconscious, but not dead; the Executioner had not dealt him a killing blow. It wasn't wise to sit for long in Nasir's presence without securing him. Bolan removed a pair of zip-tie cuffs from his pocket and secured the man's hands behind his back. Then he tied Nasir's ankles together, too, making sure the zip-ties were tight.

He found the other Dragunov and brought it over to his former vantage point. Sitting, he braced the rifle on one knee.

"Stop," Nasir said weakly.

"Too late for that now," Bolan told him.

"What are you doing?"

"Just engaging in a little justice, Nasir," Bolan said.

"I demand to know what you intend to do."

"We're just going to even the score a little." He threw the bound Nasir over his shoulder. The man was not terribly heavy, but navigating the rickety ladder from the bell tower was tricky. Bolan managed, though, and when he got to the base of the tower, he made sure the two of them had no immediate visitors.

A dead man outside the church had an old Egyptian Tokarev pistol in his belt. Bolan hefted the trusty weapon, which appeared functional and well maintained despite the loss of most of its blueing. He tucked the weapon in his belt, found the nearest jeep and threw Nasir into the passenger seat.

He found keys in the glove compartment. Starting the jeep, he directed the vehicle past the lines of dead men and the burning buildings. Thick, cloying smoke choked the air, and the smell of burned flesh was nauseating. The flamethrowers had done their terrible work each time they exploded, spreading sticky napalm everywhere, burning buildings and Padan Muka fighters alike. There were charred bodies everywhere Bolan tried to go. He did his best not to drive over them. There were certain respects one offered the dead, regardless of who those dead had been in life.

"Where are you taking me?"

"I'm just showing you the results of your handiwork," Bolan told him. "Tell me, Nasir, in all the time you were pushing people into this hellhole, did you ever once come down here? Did you ever see what you had created from within the middle of it? Or was this time you spent burning and pillaging your only real exposure to this place, when you weren't sitting in an office making life-and-death decisions based on your racist hate?"

Nasir did not try to answer.

They drove for some time. The farther they got from the edge of the ghetto, the less damage they saw, the less obvious it was combat had occurred. But as they penetrated the warren of narrow streets and makeshift buildings, the crushing, miserable conditions in which the ghetto's residents lived became that much more obvious.

The noise of the truck, the activity, the sheer novelty of a vehicle in their midst brought people out of their wood and metal shacks. They followed the jeep as Bolan beckoned to them. He had the windows down and he moved slowly, so that those who had to walk could keep up with him. He was also determined not to run anyone over accidentally. In an environment like this one, that was a real concern.

He found an area where several homes faced each other in a half circle, forming a kind of miniature town square facing a hand-dug watering hole. Several plastic buckets and jugs were arranged around the hole. Bolan could only imagine the risk of disease they were taking on by drinking that untested, most likely tainted groundwater, especially with so many people crammed so close together and using hand-dug latrines. His jaw tightened as he thought about the fact that the whole place had been completely unnecessary. He had, in the seat of the jeep next to him, the architect of the horrors arrayed before him.

He stopped and turned off the jeep. Yanking the battered Nasir out of the vehicle, he threw him onto the hood of the jeep. Then he climbed up onto the hood, stepped over Nasir and scrambled onto the roof, where he stood above the crowd.

"I speak English," he announced. "Can you understand me?"

There were many nods. Those who could not were given fast, whispered translations by those who could. The crowd watched him curiously.

"You were attacked tonight," he told the ghetto's residents. "The attack was not the fault of your government or of your countrymen." He waited while the translators hurried to catch up. "The attack was carried out by one man abusing his power, manipulating others within the government to achieve his ends. That man is here before you."

There was a collective gasp. Bolan pointed to Nasir. "This," he said, "is Nasir Muzafar, who until today was head of internal security for the prime minister. The policies that have put you in this place—" he gestured around him "—and the suffering you have endured, are because of him."

"How do we know what you say is true?" somebody asked.

"If you travel south from here—" Bolan pointed "—you'll find the battlefield. The Padan Muka attacked with flamethrowers and rifles. Many were killed. There will be survivors who make their way here. There will be many dead who do not."

Bolan looked around.

"This man, the man who has put you in this ghetto, the man who has authored the policies that oppress you, is yours to judge."

The man who had spoken before spoke again. "We do not understand. What do you want of us?"

"I don't want anything of you," Bolan said. "I want you to take this man and do as you see fit."

The ghetto denizens surged forward. They grabbed the bound, screaming Nasir and carried him off, holding him over their heads, where he squirmed in his cuffs like some sort of worm. The crowd bore him inexorably back toward the scene of the fires and the killings. When the people saw what had happened, they would be sufficiently motivated, Bolan suspected. They would do what was fitting. They would have their day, finally.

They would have their justice.

Don Pendleton
UNIFIED ACTION

A greedy financier ignites a global powder keg....

The Stony Man teams are on seemingly separate
operations in unstable regions. Able Team is
following the blood trail of mysterious military
contractors in Haiti while Phoenix Force stalks a
group of dangerous extremists in Kyrgyzstan. But
a stunning link between the two puts Stony Man
on the hunt for a ruthless financier who is plotting
a massive wave of terror—for profit.

STONY MAN®

*Available December
wherever books are sold.*

Or order your copy now by sending your name, address, zip or postal code, along with a check or
money order (please do not send cash) for $6.99 for each book ordered ($7.99 in Canada), plus
75¢ postage and handling ($1.00 in Canada), payable to Gold Eagle Books, to:

In the U.S.	**In Canada**
Gold Eagle Books	Gold Eagle Books
3010 Walden Avenue	P.O. Box 636
P.O. Box 9077	Fort Erie, Ontario
Buffalo, NY 14269-9077	L2A 5X3

Please specify book title with your order.
Canadian residents add applicable federal and provincial taxes.

**GOLD
EAGLE®**

www.readgoldeagle.blogspot.com

GSM110

Don Pendleton's Mack Bolan®

Devil's Mark

**A sinister new player hijacks
Mexico's narcotics trade....**

Trouble on the U.S.–Mexico border puts
Mack Bolan in the middle of a DEA
counternarcotics operation that's been
compromised in the worst way. The mission
takes a bizarre twist when a mysterious new
player called The Beast enters the game.
Bolan has seen enough evil to know monsters
exist and he's determined that this latest
threat will face retribution.

*Available December
wherever books are sold.*

Or order your copy now by sending your name, address, zip or postal code, along with a check or
money order (please do not send cash) for $6.99 for each book ordered ($7.99 in Canada), plus
75¢ postage and handling ($1.00 in Canada), payable to Gold Eagle Books, to:

In the U.S.	**In Canada**
Gold Eagle Books	Gold Eagle Books
3010 Walden Avenue	P.O. Box 636
P.O. Box 9077	Fort Erie, Ontario
Buffalo, NY 14269-9077	L2A 5X3

Please specify book title with your order.
Canadian residents add applicable federal and provincial taxes.

**GOLD
EAGLE**®

www.readgoldeagle.blogspot.com

GSB138

TAKE 'EM FREE
2 action-packed
novels plus a
mystery bonus

NO RISK
NO OBLIGATION
TO BUY

SPECIAL LIMITED-TIME OFFER
Mail to: Gold Eagle Reader Service

IN U.S.A.: P.O. Box 1867, Buffalo, NY 14240-1867
IN CANADA: P.O. Box 609, Fort Erie, Ontario L2A 5X3

YEAH! Rush me 2 FREE Gold Eagle® novels and my FREE mystery bonus (bonus is worth about $5). If I don't cancel, I will receive 6 hot-off-the-press novels every other month. Bill me at the low price of just $33.44 for each shipment.* That's a savings of over 15% off the combined cover prices and there is NO extra charge for shipping and handling! There is no minimum number of books I must buy. I can always cancel at any time simply by returning a shipment at your cost or by returning any shipping statement marked "cancel." Even if I never buy another book from Gold Eagle, the 2 free books and mystery bonus are mine to keep forever.

166/366 ADN E7RP

Name	(PLEASE PRINT)
Address	Apt. #
City	State/Prov.	Zip/Postal Code

Signature (if under 18, parent or guardian must sign)

Not valid to current subscribers of Gold Eagle books.
Want to try two free books from another series? Call 1-800-873-8635.

* Terms and prices subject to change without notice. Prices do not include applicable taxes. Sales tax applicable in N.Y. Canadian residents will be charged applicable provincial taxes and GST. Offer not valid in Quebec. This offer is limited to one order per household. All orders subject to approval. Credit or debit balances in a customer's account(s) may be offset by any other outstanding balance owed by or to the customer. Please allow 4 to 6 weeks for delivery. Offer available while quantities last.

Your Privacy: Worldwide Library is committed to protecting your privacy. Our Privacy Policy is available online at www.eHarlequin.com or upon request from the Reader Service. From time to time we make our lists of customers available to reputable third parties who may have a product or service of interest to you. If you would prefer we not share your name and address, please check here. ☐

Help us get it right—We strive for accurate, respectful and relevant communications. To clarify or modify your communication preferences, visit us at www.ReaderService.com/consumerschoice.

GE10